Maïstrotramountána

# Maïstrotramountána

## A KYRENIA SEA STORY

Andreas Keleshis

Translated from the Greek by
Andrew Hendry

MOUFFLON PUBLICATIONS 2007

Moufflon Publications Ltd.
20 Costi Palama
Aspelia Buildings
Apartment E1
1096 Lefkosia, Cyprus
publishing@moufflon.com.cy

www.moufflonpublications.com

First published in Greek in 2003

Copyright © 2007 Andreas Keleshis
Copyright preface © 2007 Nadia Charalambidou
All rights reserved
No part of this book may be reproduced or transmitted in any form
by any means, electronic, mechanical, photocopying, recording,
or otherwise, without the prior written permission of the publisher

ISBN 9963-642-21-7

Cover illustration by Alex Storer

Designed and typeset by Toby Macklin
Printed and bound in Cyprus by Imprinta Ltd.

# Contents

*Page 7*      Preface

*Page 13*      Maïstrotramountána

*Page 121*      Notes

*Page 127*      Kyrenia Harbour
                     *Its Boatyards, Shipowners,*
                     *Skippers & Maritime Traders*
                     *in the 19th and 20th Centuries*

# Preface

MAÏSTROTRAMOUNTÁNA is the name of a very strong northwesterly wind that lasts for many days and brings havoc in its path. It is a wind that seamen of the Mediterranean talk about in awe and do their best to avoid being caught in.

This novel describes a fishing trip that runs into such a storm. It is also, however, a celebration of the beauty of the sea in all kinds of weather, and of the landscape and seascape of Kyrenia. But *Maïstrotramountána* explores deeper issues too. It celebrates seamanship, and at the same time tells the story of a young boy's initiation into adulthood and the development of his relationships with the adults in his life, his grandfather and his uncles and, most importantly, his father. The book also traces the social and economic history of Kyrenia and its indigenous inhabitants before the Turkish invasion of 1974 – Greek Cypriot seamen and farmers mainly, and some Turkish Cypriots. This history is catalytic in the development of the port into its present form.

Most visitors to Kyrenia today see only the beautiful port and the mountain that lies behind it, Pentadaktylos. Few realize that there is far more to Kyrenia than this touristy image alone. Ironically, however, the novel starts with just such an image: Kyrenia as a still painting, serene and beautiful.

The adventure begins on a sunny winter's day, when the golden rays of the sun caress and intensify the beauty of the town resting lazily on the lap of the dark silvery-green mountain, girdled by the sea. It is against this background of calm that the storm, and the history of the town, unfold. Through the story of two catches – chapter after chapter, wave after wave – there rises to the surface in a tense narrative of extraordinary charm and suspense the history of the harbour, of its inhabitants, of its seamen and their preoccupations.

This is the first day that the sea has been calm after three weeks of stormy weather. In the fifties, when the story is set, Kyrenia was mainly a fishing harbour, but the carob trade, which accounts for the tall storehouses that surround the small port, was still active, though not on the grand scale that characterized the last decades of the 19th century and the first of the 20th. On this particular day, the fishermen of Kyrenia – of whom one is the narrator's father – are in the harbour preparing their nets to go fishing, for they are in dire need of money.

The young boy, the principal narrator, is sent to bring provisions for the trip. As he climbs up the narrow streets of the old town, he evokes through what he sees, what he feels, hears and smells, the life of the small community, its day-to-day comings and goings, and also the memories, the histories, the conditions that have shaped the old inhabitants' lives. The reader feels the stones underneath his feet, smells the scent of the earth after the rain, and tastes with the narrator the sweet preserve his grandmother offers him while he listens enchanted to the stories his grandfather tells him. The small community awakes, with its idiosyncratic characters, and the jokes and anecdotes that characterize the intimacy of life at the harbour, where everybody knows each other's business.

For the narrator, the harbour is the centre of the life of the little town. He describes the harbour at all times: quiet some mornings, busy and full of fishermen and others when the boats are getting ready to go out to sea, or when they come back full of fish; crowded when the main feasts take place, the sea feasts of Epiphany (the Baptism of Christ) in January and Kataklysmos (the flood) on the Sunday of Pentecost in late spring. Both feasts involve the blessing of the sea, an important ritual for all seafarers, as well as various sea games in which young men compete. The stories the boy's grandfather tells him, and the actual needs that arise during his fishing trips with his father, reflect the importance of the ancient trade-route links with the Greek islands of the Aegean and the history of Cypriot seafaring, skills related to the sea, the need to know the winds, the currents, the habits of the fish, the coast, and the mastering of sails, as well as the latest technological developments and their consequences. A monument of history himself, the boy's grandfather is characterized by an ideology that testifies to the politics and history of even earlier times.

The narrative has the sincerity and immediacy of a deeply felt personal account. In part this is due to the choice of a young narrator for a significant part of the narrative who is both a witness to and a protagonist in the story and who, even though the narration is retrospective, most of the time identifies with his younger self, recording perceptions and events as if experiencing them in the present. Events are described as if there is no prior knowledge of what is going to happen, nor of their ultimate outcome. As a result the present is experienced as unpredictable and unknowable, an illusion particularly important in the recounting of a sea adventure, as it lends the narrative anxiety and intensifies suspense. The illusion is intensified of perceiving the fictional world, the sea and the wind and its dangers, at the same time as the protagonist experiences it. The reader seems to feel the force of the wind on his face, the salt of seawater on his lips.

Among the great achievements of this novel are the vivid depiction of the struggle with the waves and the masterful building up of agonizing suspense as to the eventual outcome of the trip, a build-up that owes a lot to the skilful manipulation of narrative perspective as well as the sowing of almost imperceptible forebodings. World literature has known many sea adventures. Most of them concentrate on the narration of events and the description of characters. It is not often that the actual struggle with the waves is recounted and readers so nearly experience the cold seawater on their skin.

N. Charalambidou<br>
July 2006, Prodromos

FOR MY GRANDCHILDREN

*Elina, Anthea, Charis and Andreas*

# I

# Fair Weather

Etched against a blue sky, Mt Pentadaktylos gleamed in the morning light. Its peaks, streaked with various hues of rock, shimmered in the morning sun. As the sun rose, the shadows high up turned dark green, the olive trees on the slopes turned silver, and lower down, the narrow plain between the mountain and the sea began to glow a light green. The lemon trees, with their few open strips of land sown with wheat and barley, descended the hillsides to merge with the steep and occasionally inaccessible coastline. The headlands, in some places high and in others low, embraced the bays exposed to the north wind and then plunged or gradually receded into the deep blue sea.

Nestling snugly in the middle of the scene lay the small town with – at the very centre of the picture – its harbour, spreading out in the shadow of the tall castle. The sketch's well-drawn lines, clearly and boldly executed, never altered. Only the hues changed, the shading, the tones, in accordance with the time, the day, the season, and the light of the sun that gradually wheeled overhead. The light of the sun which at dusk, before it disappeared, cast all its warmest tones over towards the edge of the sketch, in front of the church of the Glykiotissa,[1] with the island lying just off the coast, bathing everything in view – the sky, the clouds, the mountain and the sea.

How fortunate were those who had stood on the waterfront next to the endless constantly murmuring waves and tasted the saltiness of the *maïstros*[2] blowing in from the sea, watching the sunset – especially those occurring at about the time of the two equinoxes, when the sun went down between the mainland and Snake Island.[3]

I strolled casually along the waterfront with my friends; the schools had broken up for the Christmas holiday. It was a warm and sunny day, without the slightest breeze; at our feet the sea seemed unusually calm, while off to the left Kombonisi Island[4] looked as if it had been cemented over, with the sea around it hard and whitened. We made for the harbour, walked along the mole and climbed up the lighthouse steps. This was our favourite haunt, the place where we always finished our continual discussions; we had many cares at that time but we always, almost always, took the right decisions. The place itself helped, with its peaceful surroundings.

In this small town there were lots of things to do and lots of places you could go to on feast-days. The sea, the mountain, the houses, relatives and friends, people in general, were all close at hand. It didn't take long to get anywhere, everything was so close and so intimate. Tomorrow we would go up the mountain, to St Hilarion,[5] to the castle with the hundred houses of the Rígena,[6] as we did every year at this time. It was an easy decision to make: we'd set out from the plane tree, early next morning at seven.

We were coming down the lighthouse steps when we saw a figure running towards us: it was Kotchis, our Dimitrakis, who was always eager, though nature had treated him unkindly. He was mentally and physically backward; he hadn't developed as he should have done, and would always remain a child. When he reached us, he took me by the hand.

'Go right now, Christakis says. Your friends can go too.'

We all understood what he meant. We all hurried to get round to the other side of the harbour. On the sand beneath the castle the harbour folk had gathered and were preparing to launch the fishing boats out to sea. They had no time to lose; they had to seize this opportunity for the weather was incredibly calm and winter catches were always good ones. God had not forsaken them: it was nearly three weeks since they'd last had work, they had no ready cash to buy food with; they were finding it hard to make ends meet, and they were all heavily in debt. A festival was coming up, and festivals are an expensive business: how would they celebrate Christmas, only four days away? This moon brought only storms, but now, four days before it was due to disappear, the sea had fortunately grown calm.

The first boat to be prepared was the *Astero*, which belonged to my Uncle Charalámbis. About ten people on each side, all in high spirits and boosted by the calm weather, held it erect and began to push it, amusing themselves with the chant of 'yele-yele-yele'[7] that echoed all around the harbour. They would stop only when a wooden slipper was released. Then somebody would grab the slipper and place it under the keel of the stern.

'Feed it in nicely now ... mind the rudder,' cried Pateras,[8] whose job was to keep an eye on the slippers and grease them with sheep's fat so that the keel could slide smoothly over them.

As soon as the stern entered the water, my other uncle, Savvas, took off his shoes and trousers, got into the water in his white underpants and climbed onto the boat. The harbour echoed with hoots and whistles. Before long half of Kyrenia had gathered. Women holding children in their arms gazed on the scene from the terrace at Trypití,[9] high up above the sea, opposite the harbour mouth. When it was the turn of our boat, the loveliest of all, as soon as it entered the water I jumped in, holding my shoes in my hand. I didn't have to take off my trousers as I was wearing shorts. This didn't go down at all well with the local riffraff, who had also been enlivened by the calm weather.

'Hey, Christaki, aren't you ashamed of yourself, letting the young lad freeze like that?'

'Haven't you seen enough bare arses for one day?' he retorted. 'Don't tell me you want to see another one!'

The local riffraff were a permanent group of five or six individuals who had never worked but always managed to make ends meet, and almost all of them were well-dressed and respectable-looking. They fell in with the few tourists and foreigners who passed through, both male and female, and, as the occasion demanded, transformed themselves effortlessly into poor students, rich people who had no need to work, ship's captains, or sorry individuals who despaired of love and life. Only when things got tough were they forced to work, and then they got onto the boats as fishermen's hands – 'as casual labourers,' they said. Recently the harbour had had the misfortune to lose one of them. A plump and wealthy middle-aged English woman, daubed with make-up and perfume, had passed through, seized him and carried him off... 'Wish us good luck too!' cried those who were left behind.

I put the oars in the rowlocks and went and tied up the *Argo* – that was her name – in her berth, over the way by the steps, next to the *Astero*. Before long all of the boats were in the water. The harbour had come to life, the coffee-houses and the quays had filled with people. The sheds around the bay had opened and the fishermen were carrying nets, long-lines[10] and buoy-lines. The air was full of the harbour folk's banter. I was still stacking the slippers away under the foredeck when my father arrived.

'Nip over to the shed, pick up the two metal petrol cans and go on home. Tell your mother to pack some food for us and to sort out some thick clothes for you, we're going to be away all night. While she's getting everything ready, run over to Simos's pumps and get him to fill up the cans. Tell him to keep a note of it. Everybody's going to set their nets close to the harbour. But I'm not going to waste a calm sea like this; I've got fresh bait – picarel and cuttlefish – which Mitros sent me today from Lefkosia. We'll risk it, we'll go about eleven miles out[11] ... in the sea off Pig Island[12] there's a reef hardly anyone knows about which hasn't been fished.'

His dream of making a big catch, especially in the winter, had never left him. It would revive during the enforced idleness of stormy days and grow during the frequent blasts of the *tramountana*[13] in winter. It was at such times that he dreamed of unknown, virgin fishing banks ideal for long-lines, reefs full of coral rock, unfished, with large fish roaming around. When the first spell of calm weather came, he was always ready, waiting to make the big catch.

From the moment he'd come down to the sea to work as a fisherman, I'd been helping him out. From the age of ten, during the summer and in the holidays, I'd worked as a sailor for him. The rest of the time he fished on his own. He was more of a long-line fisherman; he wasn't that keen on nets. Now he was in a hurry. Without saying a word, I jumped out of the boat, grabbed his bicycle and took it up to the raised terrace of Trypití, with the narrow passage that cuts through the tall houses and brings you straight out into the heart of the Old Town. Our shed was up there, next to the church of the Chrysopolitissa. I hung the petrol cans on the rack at the back of the bike and set off for home.

Five years earlier we'd bought a house outside the Old Town – 'in a hell of a bad spot' some folks said, about a kilometre from the harbour, on the broad road that led to Lefkosia, in the area my ma had liked when my father first brought her here, fifteen years before. Both sides of the road were lined with these strange big trees, which became weighed down with bunches of mauve flowers in spring, even before the trees began to sprout leaves, and which sometimes flowered again before winter.

My father had borrowed three hundred pounds, just for two or three months. But then suddenly everything went wrong… he fell ill, had a spell in hospital and then on medication… he closed his shop… He was lucky for within a year he'd found another job with a large company in another town. But the indomitable spirit inside him couldn't stand being ordered around, and on the third day he flew into a rage, beat the living daylights out of his boss and returned to his roots… the sea. Meanwhile the debt mounted up and my ma was forced to take up sewing.

'Is that you, son? Shall I get you something to eat?' said my ma, and she got up, putting the dress she was sewing down on the chair. Last night she'd sewn all night long; it was Christmas in four days' time and she had to have everything ready. I quickly explained the situation to her.

'The blessed sea is calm,' she murmured, and she set about preparing the things her husband had asked for. 'Nip out to the bakery and get two loaves. Your little brother has vanished today, he'll be roaming round the orchards with his catapult, and I've sent your sister to deliver a dress; I hope they pay her for it.'

By the time I got back, she'd got everything ready, and she also slipped in a loaf for me. She tied everything – clothes, food, the lot – into a big bundle and handed it to me with a look of deep affection.

'God be with you, son, take care.'

She had a heart of gold, my ma, she'd never once complained, and I'd never heard her raise her voice; she believed in God's providence, and she always placed her trust in Him. And yet I knew for a fact that her life hadn't always been like this; until just five years ago she'd been comfortably off – I could remember it clearly; I too could recall those days.

When I reached the harbour, my old man was sitting on the steps baiting to a strong long-line[14] and chatting to his brothers Charalámbis and Savvas, who were in the *Astero*, ready to set out to sea as well. They were in a hurry because their nets had to be set before sunset; they wanted to make two catches, one in the evening and one at dawn. Their uncle, Kapetán Panayís, the brother of their old man, who'd passed away, was watching them, leaning against a marble bollard. The three of them had been my father's teachers; it was they who had taught him the craft.

I stood next to the old sea-dog; as soon as his gaze met mine, he put his arm around my shoulder.

'So, my young salt, you're going to go out with the big man ... if he yells at you, just laugh ... that's what we're like in our family, we're a lively bunch.'

My ma used to say more or less the same thing: they're no lambs, you know, they're lions; let them get worked up, it suits them, just make sure that when they're in a temper you don't pay attention to what they say and don't talk back; leave them alone, they calm down easily by themselves.

They were real mountains of men, all of them big-boned and stoutly-built, with loud voices and quick tempers; nobody dared to argue with them, nor would anybody try and calm them down when they were angry. It was just the way they were, my ma used to say.

The two older ones, now aged between fifty and fifty-five, had travelled together since they were boys, first as sailors and later as boatswains with their old man Kapetán Michalis, and then later still with their uncle, Kapetán Panayís. By now they should have been skippers of caiques. Savvas, the eldest, had been with his old man on the schooner that was sunk by the French in the Great War, when they were on their way back from Rhodes.

My old man had never travelled on the tall-masted ships. Only once, one summer, was he taken by his father to the *panegyri*[15] of Chrysosotiros church, at Akanthou.[16] The big two-masted schooner had been full of people, most of them relatives; he could recall the cries of the women whenever the schooner leaned over to one side. He also had hazier recollections of races that used to take place between the caiques, a bit like yacht races. He was very young when his old man died; they, his brothers, had brought him up lovingly, even if they had called him 'titch'. They had taken over the helm; they'd stood by the whole family, making sure they lacked for nothing and that the household stood firm. They'd helped their mother and married off their sisters.

'Bring the boat up close,' ordered my old man, putting aside the long-line and pretending not to have heard his uncle. 'We'll load all the gear on board and I'll carry on baiting the line after we've set out. We've got a two-hour journey ahead of us.'

As the *Astero* set off, I drew the boat alongside the jetty and held it there until he had loaded all the gear on board – long-lines, buoy-lines, lamps, petrol, clothes and food.

'Have you filled the *koukoumara*[17] with fresh water?' he asked me as he got in.

I grabbed hold of the small pitcher that was stowed away under the bow-seat, jumped out of the boat and filled it with fresh water from the tap at the top of the steps. I got back into the boat, started up the engine, pushed the boat away from the side of the jetty and sat at the helm.

'You've got a good sailor there, Christaki,' his uncle, Kapetán Panayís, called down to us, 'but, like we said, it's winter and you can't trust the weather. In winter, together with storms we get the finest days of the year, but don't forget that this calm weather will only last for two or three days at the most.'

His voice sounded heavy and hoarse, as if he was a long way off. He leaned on his stick and set off for home; he limped up the Trypití steps and then disappeared.

# 2

# The Old Ships

HE FELT A DEEP AFFECTION and respect for his uncle, Kapetán Panayís. He always heeded his words. He was my grandfather's brother, the last of Kyrenia's famous captains, the last senior captain on Severis' ships.[18] I admired him too: everything I knew about the sea, about Kyrenia's ships and her sailors, I had learnt from him. From a young age I had been a regular caller at his home.

Like all the old seafarers, he lived in the narrow streets of the Old Town, the only town that had an island flavour, the flavour of the Aegean islands. Nearly all those who lived in its narrow lanes were related to each other and had age-old ancestral ties with the sea. It was a small close-knit community that led a harmonious life closely tied to the local area, the harbour and the sea. Everyone else, all those who lived outside, were regarded as land-lubbers and almost foreigners.

'Have you come to see us again, poppet? Have you missed your old uncle, or my sweet?' my great aunt Maritsoú, his wife, would ask with a smile.

'Both,' I would reply.

She liked the answer I gave her: she knew I was being honest, that I liked her sweet and the way she used to serve it – reddish-yellow coils of bitter orange stuck on the end of a fork and placed in a glass of water. It had a sweet smell of scented geraniums, as did all of her garden, which was full of flowers planted in tins, in lentisk compost brought from the island of the Glykiotissa, Snake Island.

We used to sit behind the gate leading into the small courtyard. As he lay back in his deckchair and I sat on a cane stool,[19] I would listen to him talking about different types of weather and seas and faraway ports. The Levant, the Black Sea, the whole of the Aegean would unfold before my eyes and spread out over the small paved courtyard ... its stone slabs began to assume the forms of islands and ports.

The small slab at my feet was Kastellorizo, always the first and the last leeward anchorage; another, large slab to the left was Rhodes; above it was Smyrna, and higher up, above all the others – the only marble slab – was Constantinople. Further down, in the middle of the yard, was the famous port of Syros, lower still was Piraeus and at the very bottom lay a rough, long and narrow firestone: Crete. Good for Crete, he would often say, at last she'd managed to achieve permanent union with Greece.

Apart from the sea, he had another passion, a great longing to enter Kyrenia harbour in his schooner with the blue-and-white flag[20] flying from his stern, just as it did in his heart, and flying there permanently, not merely hoisted on the foremast for a few days every year whenever he entered a Greek port.

Once he'd believed that such a time was close at hand. He had become convinced of the fact after that unforgettable voyage to Smyrna, on the first anniversary of its liberation, in the middle of May 1920.

He had been anchored in the middle of the harbour and had seen the ships there decked out with flags, with their sailors lining the bows; he had heard the cannon-shots and the doxology at the church of Ayia Fotiní, and he had joined the huge throng of people who were celebrating wildly on the quay, laughing, crying and waving banners.

On that day he had believed, he had been sure that at last the time had come: soon Ayia Sophia and then ... then the flag that he loved so dearly would arrive, entering his island through the beautiful port of Kyrenia, for it was the only port – there was no other on the whole of the island.

The streets, the quays, the piers would be decked out with flags and strewn with myrtle and laurel leaves, and the fiery bishop would be waiting motionless, cross in hand, on the main quay ... But how would the whole of that fleet be able to fit into the little harbour? ... He reckoned, he imagined that only one ship would enter, one decked out with flags, with the King on board and its sailors saluting, and it would anchor by the Koula,[21] while the others remained outside.

Just two years later, however, the dream came to an end, in an awful way. Hard times followed, the years of the Asia Minor Disaster, years of forced evacuation, sadness and pain. Many ships came into the harbour, but they bore no flags, only holds bursting with tears and pain, with refugees. The small town embraced all these souls, all this human flotsam anzd jetsam, sharing in their pain ... He was saddened, disillusioned and wept ... After that another ten years had passed, and after a long wait, in the uprising of 1931, when Cyprus first rose up to demand her freedom, he had been unable to resist and had joined in the revolt as well. The English had thrown him in prison.

A year before, on New Year's Eve, he had sent for me early in the morning and I had gone to his house. He had been expecting me: he handed me a cloth bag, took his stick and we went out into the street. 'We're going to the cemetery,' he told me, 'to light the lamp at their grave ... it's a bit of a walk ... we'll take it steady.'

He was a hale and hearty man, sturdy and broad-shouldered, with a round face, straight hair and bright eyes behind his round glasses. He limped a little but set a good pace, despite his seventy-seven years. He limped, or rather sprang up suddenly, as if in pain, whenever the whole weight of his body fell onto his left foot. We left the narrow lanes behind us and came out onto the broad east road with its tall cypresses, which led out of town towards Aï-Grosi.[22] Only once, half way along, did he need to stop for a few moments.

The roads were wet, the wind smelled of earth and wet grass, and the leaves were still dripping. There had been a storm at dawn but now the sun had come out and was shining cheerfully. It was keen to dry the wet earth, aided by a light breeze from the east which began to break yellow and brown leaves off the trees and scatter them over the narrow glistening asphalt surface of the road. Most of them were leaves from almond trees, and they whirled round and round, glistening in the morning sun; all of them had to come down for the bare branches to bring forth new blossom a few days later.

When we arrived, I opened the iron gate and he went in. He walked past the statues and the marble crosses on top of the tombs of the wealthy, carried straight on for about twenty paces and stopped on the left at a faded white wooden cross fastened to a huge cypress tree, with a rusty cut-up tin can at its foot. The names engraved on the cross had worn away.

He took the bag out of my hand and asked me to fetch him some water. When I returned he was kneeling down, clearing the grave of weeds. He sprinkled some water over the wet earth, rinsed out the clay oil-lamp that lay under the can, put a little water in it, filled it with some of the oil that we had brought with us and placed it carefully at the foot of the cross. With trembling hands he put a new flaxen wick in it and lit it ... He stood up, leaned against the cypress for a few moments with his hand on the cross and then kneeled down again. He took seven candles out of the bag, planted them in the wet earth and lit them. A tear rolled down his cheek.

Here, together with his grandmother, lay the body of his grandfather, Kapetán Turkomíchalos, a real mountain of a man, who had fled from his island after killing two men. A persecuted wretch, the sea had cast him up at Kyrenia. He liked the wildness of the sea and the beauty of the place, saying it was like his own island of Cythera. Perhaps Aphrodite deceived him: he was well acquainted with the goddess, who up until then he had thought was a native of Cythera and not Cyprus. He put down his roots, produced sturdy male shoots and filled the port with sons who became experienced seamen and captains ... The sons became grandsons ... The grandsons became great-grandsons ... He knew only one trade – seafaring, and had only one love – the sea; the tiller was constantly under his arm.

Yet this mercurial sea had devoured three of his four seafaring sons: Kapetán Gliyóris, who was lost at Sounion; Kapetán Aléxandros, at Cape Gata near Limassol; and, last of all, Kapetán Andonis, who was drowned in the sea off Symi, in that freezing cold January of 1885 – the same accursed year in which the big three-masted ship *Ta Tria Adelfia*[23] was wrecked outside Smyrna, and then a little later, in May, Kapetán Piklíyiannis' ship, after setting out from Anamur. The small town was draped in black that accursed year.

In this spot was later buried his old man, Kapetán Savvas, Turkomíchalos' eldest son, the only one to be laid in the ground, together with Anna, his mother. Now he really was what you would call a captain. His name was well-known in every port, even those on the Black Sea. He knew better than anyone else how to read the signs of the weather; rarely was he caught off guard by storms or northerly gales ... 'It's the most important thing in seamanship,' he would say time and time again. They called him 'the Sea Master' as he took great pleasure in teaching others: apart from his three sons, he produced many other captains.

Later his elder brother, Kapetán Michalis, was buried here, together with his wife Markaroú. He had been their old man, the great teacher's pride and joy: a noble figure, tough, strong, a real sea dog; few rode the waves as he could. Deep down he bore a strange love for the sea. The sea and only the sea dominated his life, with its fearsome power ... he had no need of any other kind of company.

Here, a few years before, his other brother, Alexis, had also been buried. It was here that he himself wanted to be buried when the time came; he was awaiting the moment when he could lie down beside them, to become part of the same earth, to be reunited with them.

The small town's seafarers had been proud and famous sea dogs. In everyone's thoughts and minds they always took pride of place, with their schooners and goletas,[24] their rigging, long bowsprits and tall masts. Single-masted, two-masted and even three-masted ships, driven by the power of the wind and nothing but sails – lateen sails, mainsails and jibs[25] – seamanship and sharp wits, had been roving around the Levant for centuries, controlling the island's trade. The art of seamanship passed from father to son, and from old man to young. Some were captains and merchants at the same time. From Kyrenia, but more often from the southern ports, Larnaca and Limassol, they would set sail in southerly and easterly directions for Alexandria, Jaffa and Beirut, or make for the ports of Mersin, Anamur and Antalya. Sailing close to the *maïstros*, they would sail towards the Aegean islands, Smyrna, Syros, and Piraeus; they would enter the straits, make for Constantinople and then head for the ports of the Black Sea.

Yet, however much they loved the seas of the Levant, with their calm waters, ancient ports and eastern Mediterranean sea lanes, their great loves, the places with which they had special ties, were the Aegean, Asia Minor, Constantinople and Sebastopol. Wherever there were Greeks, they had relatives, friends and associates. Above all, they loved the Aegean.

The Aegean was not a love, it was a romance, a passion. Their greatest joy and pleasure was to sail around the Aegean, with its innumerable islands, in which each island, each barren isle, each rocky islet had a story and a myth of its own. A truly idyllic Aegean, full of valiant gods, mermaids and saints, with ports, havens and leeward anchorages for all types of weather. From there, with the *maïstros* and dolphins for company, the ancient route to the homeland was not only easy, it was a delight … Sailing directly before the wind or at broad reach, one hoped the last stretch of the return journey would never end, especially once the Pentadaktylos mountains hove into view and the peak of St Hilarion stood out clearly.

The lofty warehouses beneath the houses with the high wooden balconies, the wharves and the jetties used to fill up with piles of merchandise: dried fruit, buttery pulses, *touloumotyria*,[26] timber, hides and many other types of goods, all brought from the north, along the trade routes of the *maïstros* and the *tramountána*. The coffee-houses and the harbour would fill with sailors, porters, merchants from Lefkosia and idlers. Loaded carts and donkeys would ceaselessly come and go. Caiques would leave the small town loaded with whatever the local land produced: oil, carobs, cotton, wheat and barley, olive-cake, patterned cotton cloth, dyed clothes and an occasional jackass. At the southern ports, for the *levante* and *ostria*[27] trade routes, they would load barrels of wine, oil and carobs and bring back dates, spices, oil and petrol in cans. During the days of sail, through difficult times, for centuries, the island's trade lay in the holds of the ships from the beautiful port.

The port, however, gradually fell into decline and began to die a slow death. The famous tall-masted ships with their long bowsprits grew fewer and fewer and eventually disappeared. Along with them disappeared the old sea dogs.

The boatbuilders, too, scattered and disappeared. First Mastro-Fytós and his brothers left for Limassol, then Mastro-Matthaios for Famagusta, and Mastro-Vasilis, the best apprentice, for Karavostasi. Mastro-Panáos and Mastro-Pandelís tried hard to stay for they had come to love the people and the town which had once welcomed them as refugees. Karkánias, the famous craftsman, stopped making anchors, chains, shroud plates and hawse-hole plates,[28] closed his forge at Tsiakkilerí[29] and disappeared like the others. They were all driven away by need; the craftsmen and the apprentices all left, the shipyards and the dockyards closed down, and Tsiakkilerí was abandoned.

The ships with the tall masts and long bowsprits have scattered and disappeared and no longer exist. The last vessel to be built, the last ship to be set up on the stocks, that belonging to the shipowner Savvas Charalambous, stood abandoned as an empty frame at Tsiakkilerí for years until it was turned into firewood.

The last ship, a small, white single-masted schooner belonging to Kapetán Matthaios, which stood out of the water at Tsiakkilerí for years, was launched into the sea about ten years ago, unfurled its sails and sailed away without ever returning.

The seasoned old captains are gradually dying out; only four of them are left, grounded old wrecks, captains confined to shore without caiques. Kapetán Matthaios doesn't even come down to the harbour any more; neither does Kapetán Neoklís, who somehow manages to hobble up into the foothills to gaze at Anamur ... to cast anchor. Kleanthís' son, Kostís, the last sailmaker, looks after a rich man's yacht, which lies permanently at anchor by the Koula.

The other chief captain, Kapetán Panayís, tried to hold out for a while longer. After the tall-masted ships had disappeared, he turned to building lighters, which Kostís, Kleanthís' son, rigged with lateen sails. He began to carry cargoes of carobs to ships lying outside the harbour but he soon realized that it was no job for a captain ... without the sea ... without seeing the open sea ... the Aegean. He was unable to bear it any longer and he called in his relative Charalambis, who took out a bottomry loan and took over the lighters and the business.

Everything that was achieved through the experience of so many generations, over the course of so many years, is now disappearing; everything, even the boatswains along with the sailors. Nobody splices ropes any more, either for rigging, for sails, or for hawsers. The ancient marble bollards on the harbour wharves remained bare, without hawsers; they have disappeared and all become a thing of the past. Only the houses with their high balconies are left, standing with an air of faded nobility and all those who dwell in them have a dreamy look, as if they live with their memories of the past.

Nowadays the young people, if they don't leave, become lightermen or fishermen and together with the summer visitors, the Aegean sponge-divers with their Aegean *trehantiria*[30] and the carob export trade, restore to the beautiful port a little of its former glory. Occasionally a foreign caique arrives, with a low mast though no sails. It anchors in the middle of the harbour and fills it with squared lengths of timber. Even more rarely, a Siphnian boat will moor alongside the wharf of the Customs House and unload earthenware pots. These days very few of the lofty warehouses, wharves and jetties fill up with goods, and when they do it is only for a short while and only with carobs.

Along with the harbour the small town itself has also fallen into decline. Its shipowners and captains have lost their trade and seafaring is on the wane. The trouble began during the Great War when the ships were unable to put into Turkish ports as at that time the country was everybody's enemy. Later, the relatives, friends and associates who lived there, hard-working country and sea folk, were wiped out. On the other hand, steel-built ships driven by engines were becoming more and more common, yet they preferred more southerly and profitable routes; they didn't put in at Kyrenia and in any case were too big to fit into the small harbour. Another, large harbour was constructed at Famagusta, and they would go and dock there.

The age-old harbour here has remained small, just as it always has been, with the ancient Koula in the middle, its two wooden wharves and its two jetties stretching out to enfold it, leaving the harbour mouth open to the *tramountána*. Small, yet always so beautiful. Rarely had the sea grown as calm and still as it had on this particular day, like a sheet of glass, without a single ripple. All year long without ceasing, except for a few days during the winter, the *maïstros* blows, caressing and washing the shores, the bays, the coves and the headlands with gentle waves. It begins each morning as a gentle breeze, grows in strength as the day wears on, begins to abate in the afternoon, and then as the sun goes down it settles, and a little while later the waves it has created settle too. At about midnight a gentle breeze begins to blow down from Mt Pentadaktylos, the *katevatós*, which lasts until morning, until the *maïstros* begins to blow again. The sea current, which is also steady, almost all year round moves downwards, in an easterly direction.

Yet this sea, this beautiful sea, is not to be trifled with. If it gets angry and suddenly and unexpectedly begins to foam, the waves whipped up by the *tramountána* rise up, break out in the open sea and crash furiously down onto the rocks, which wince and howl with pain, then ride over the jetties, the foot of the lighthouse and the surrounding roads and burst into the harbour, whose mouth lies open to the full force of the *tramountána*. At times like this no vessel can escape its fury, no matter whether it is inside or outside the harbour. It is sheer hell, and yet incredibly majestic.

It always bursts in at night and resembles an earthquake, always strongest on the first day, in the first few hours. When dawn breaks it gradually begins to lose strength, but when the hour it first burst in comes round again it blows up once more and gains strength. Gradually, hour by hour, day by day, within three, four or five days, it loses strength, subsides and eventually dies out.

How many caiques, how many souls, how many boats, how many dreams, how many households have been wrecked ... The last wreck, that of Salisvourís' caique,[31] with torn beams and frame, as if ripped apart by the teeth of some monster, lies gaping beneath the castle as a reminder of the terrible fury of the sea when it is whipped up by the *tramountána*. How many disasters, how many misfortunes, how much sadness has been brought by this *tramountána* ... this north wind ...

# 3

# A Moonless Passage

All sailors love the moon; they take it into account and rely upon it. Fishermen, however, do not; they take it into account, but they have no love for it and do not want it, particularly on nights around the time of the full moon. They prefer dark moonless nights so that the nets, fish traps and long-lines cannot be seen on the sea-bed. Fish can see well at night.

Fishermen love only one kind of moon: the midsummer, August moon; the warmest, the biggest and the most beautiful. For its sake they do not work on the days on which it appears, nor do they fish on the nights when it shines. In the old days they used to go out into the open sea and keep it company as it sailed in full glory over Pentadaktylos.

'Keep to the headlands, don't go out to sea or too close to the shore, we'll take the shortest route,' said my old man, scarcely before we had left the harbour. 'It's half past one, we're late … today is the shortest day of the year. Head the boat towards Chrysokava Bay.'

He fetched two strong long-lines for deep water and a fine one for shallow water. Each strong long-line had a hundred and fifty hooks. Its short monofilament[32] branch-lines, each of which was about ninety centimetres. long and had a large hook at the end, were fastened at intervals of about ten metres[33] to the thick mono-filament main-line, which was a mile long. The main-line and the branch-lines were skilfully and methodically laid in a round shallow cane basket, with the hooks pinned onto a layer of cork around the rim of the basket. When the line was set it sank down to the seabed, with its ends fastened to the buoys, which were left to float on the surface of the sea.

He laid the long-line on top of the engine cover and carried on baiting it, pulling the hooks out of the cork one by one and baiting them with picarel.

'What's the date today?' he asked.

'December the twenty-first. Why?'

'Tonight is the longest night of the year. Do you know how many days old the moon is? Do you know how to find out?' He assumed a serious air. 'It's very important for sailors and fishermen ... I'll teach you ... listen ... there's a starting-point – the 'base number' – and to find it you have to add eleven to the base number for the previous year. Whenever the new total comes to over thirty, you subtract thirty. This year (1951) the base number is twenty-two, and to this you add the date and the month, plus one. If the result is also over thirty, then again you subtract thirty, and what you are left with is the age of the moon.'

'That means today ... the moon is twenty-six days old,'[34] I said, quickly doing the calculation.

'That's right, you'll just be able to see a thin sliver, it'll be a moonless night, really good for fishing. In two days' time there'll be a new moon, at Christmas, that is.'

He had told me about this before but always forgot that he had done so. Each time the explanation was accompanied by a strange sadness ... Whenever he talked about the moon, he remembered his old man, Kapetán Michalis ... the saddest memory of his life was revived.

On that spring morning, a few days after Easter, his old man had taken him by the hand and led him away. Although he was young, he was surprised because the tough skipper was not given to displaying his affections. They went down to the harbour, which that day smelled neither of pitch, fish or carobs. The winter had gone, the sweet smell of spring was in the air, and the crag martins had returned to their old nests high up in the castle and were flying about fishing for food overhead, ceaselessly proclaiming the arrival of spring.

The harbour was full of boats, most of them anchored in the middle, while others were moored alongside the two wharves. All of them were freshly done up and painted, with spruced-up sails and rigging and freshly caulked and tarred bottoms. Men, donkeys and ox-carts came and went; together with the porters, the crews engaged for the return journeys carried provisions for the voyage, wooden barrels full of water, merchandise, suitcases and passengers' trunks. Some of these were piled up on the wharves and others in the ships' boats. It was the time of year when people began to travel; ships would set sail for other towns on the island such as Larnaca and Limassol, and for other ports, such as those in the Levant, the Aegean and the Black Sea. All the captains were present; only he was shorebound. The English had not allowed him to board ship since the time his two-masted schooner *Evangelistria* had been sunk by the French navy, back in the Great War.

It had been a few days before Christmas, he was anchored in Rhodes harbour and was unloading the olive-cake he'd taken on board in Kyrenia. Once he had finished unloading, that same day, the Italians forced him to leave the harbour. He had no choice but to set sail in the middle of winter for his homeland, with fine weather and a small cargo of soap. At the end of the following day, however, a rough sea, with small choppy and uneven waves, forced him to change course. Despite the slackness of the wind, through a long series of manoeuvres and admirable seamanship he managed to avoid the numerous barren islets and reefs and during the night succeeded in entering and tying up in the deep harbour of Kastellorizo.

Very early next morning, however, he was driven out of there as well by the French navy: they towed him out of the harbour by force. He unfurled his sails once more and headed in the direction of Kyrenia. As he had feared, though, the choppy sea turned into a heavy swell from the north which grew much rougher, throwing up mountainous waves. The worst thing of all was the feeble wind, which was much too weak for the sails, leaving them limp and ineffective. Four days and nights he battled with the waves of the northern swell; above all, he struggled to prevent them from driving him off course to the Barbary Coast,[35] further south.

On the morning of the fourth day, some greyish-blue mountains appeared in the distance and then, very clearly, the shores of Paphos: he'd made it, the waves had not driven him far off course, yet a little further and he would have missed the island. Two hours before sundown the old sea dog managed to draw near the shore; he found a good haven outside Paphos, behind the reefs of Mouliá, so he made his way there and dropped anchor. He intended to wait there until the weather had settled and the swell had died down.

'You'll be celebrating Christmas at home,' he promised his sailors, who were overcome with exhaustion. 'Tomorrow the swell will die down and the waves will begin to drop; they'll be calmed by the *maïstros* that'll come in,' he said, gazing now at the foaming, roaring sea and now at the mainland.

Bad luck continued to dog him, however; the curse of Rhodes remained. That very afternoon, one hour before the sun went down over the boundless sea off Paphos, another French warship, the *Pothuau*, one of the many that patrolled the Levant during the Great War, saw him, sent a whale-boat with a boarding party ... arrested him ... put the sailors on shore ... and planted dynamite on the schooner.

The beautiful vessel, tired but unsubdued by the waves, lay at anchor with its bow facing into the north wind and was proudly swaying from side to side. Its rusted anchor holes in the sides of the bow, like large tearful eyes, gazed at the shores of Paphos, waiting for the weather to change, for the *maïstros* to blow, to set sail for Kyrenia.

Suddenly the sea erupted, the Mouliá rocks shook, the reefs shuddered. Jets of foam mixed with pieces of mast, spars, rigging, wooden beams and sails shot high up into the air ... and the sea was filled with wreckage. The broken shell of the schooner, what was left of it, slowly sank with a strange air of solemnity and disappeared beneath the shallow waters of the Mouliá.

They took him, clapped in irons, to Kastellorizo, where for days they tortured him to try and get him to confess, to admit things he had never done ... Later, in Paris, the trial took place in his absence ... They adjudged the sinking of the *Evangelistria* to have been a legitimate act and they condemned him to death on the false charge that he had been supplying German submarines with oil ... Later they transferred him from Kastellorizo to Egypt and they handed him over to the English for execution, seeing as he was a British subject.

The English did not really believe the story and they shut him up in a prisoner-of-war camp, for they were all too familiar with the well-known sloppiness and disorganization of the French. They carried out their own investigation in their own systematic fashion. The truth came out; first they spared his life and then they set him free. However, they still found a few false pretexts to avoid having to pay him compensation, and they ordered him to remain ashore ... the investigations, they said, were continuing.

He sank into despair. Another spring came round ... how long would he, a chief captain, from a family of famous chief captains, have to remain without a ship, cut off from the open sea?

He and his father boarded the *Archángelos*, the two-masted ship belonging to his father's first cousin Poupás,[36] who was moored alongside the Customs House wharf loading goods. That moment a single-masted schooner drew away from the steps leading down from the wharf to the sea. The anchor was raised and the schooner's boat, with its crew at the four oars, began to tow it. The small boat continued to tow the ship until it had passed through the harbour mouth. Then the boat was lifted aboard the schooner, which unfurled its sails – first the mainsail and then the jib – then headed out into the *tramountána* and began to move away.

They got off his cousin's ship and went over to the coffee-house opposite, while Kapetán Michalis gazed constantly at the ship that was sailing away. He sat his son next to him, took a piece of string out of his pocket and murmured, 'Let me see if you can remember how to make a bowline knot. It's the most important knot for sailors.'

When he was satisfied, he began to explain to his son how to find out the age of the moon. The coffee and Turkish delight they had ordered arrived, the old sea dog picked up the coffee cup, took a sip and then ... gradually began to tip over ... and as he tipped over he breathed his last ... his eyes still wide open, fixed on the ship which was leaning in the wind and moving further and further away with its sails full open.

Everybody said at the time that his soul had departed just in time, for suddenly a *garbís*[37] blew up, the single-masted ship turned, caught the fresh breeze sideways-on, leaned over further, became encircled by foam and sailed away close to the wind in a north-westerly direction. Its two sails billowed out as if they were an archangel's wings, just like those of the Archangel Michael in the icon in his church above the harbour ... later, the dolphins came and accompanied it on its journey to the Aegean.

When he had finished baiting the first long-line, he stood gazing for a while at the mountain, the mainland and the sea, and he sighed. He slowly put on a thick blue overcoat – the *partesou*,[38] as he called it, a relic from the good old days – and fetched another long-line.

'Come on, put on a pair of long trousers and a jacket, otherwise you'll catch cold.'

I put on the old clothes which had once been his. I folded the sleeves and the trouser-legs up about three or four times as they were much too big for me; I must have looked like a scarecrow. He began baiting again.

'Yesterday I saw Kazinieris[39] ... he's one of us,' he said.

I realized what he was getting at and so I tried to sidetrack him and take his mind off the subject.

'I know,' I said, 'he's from a family of seafarers, like us.'

'His old man was a stranger in Kyrenia, from the mountains; Hadji-Gliyóris brought him here for his casino.[40] Later, though, he did well for himself, then fell in love with the sea and came to own his own boat ... Some time later he married Kapetán Pagonis' daughter.'

'The other day when you sent me to his house I saw a really beautiful silver boat hanging over the door, with sails and rigging. It had a transom stern, like the *Argo*'s.'

'That's the *Pombarta*,[41] the boat his old man used to have. His family, though, was ruined and declared itself bankrupt ... they put everything under the hammer, even the furniture ... that was a long time ago, before the harbour began to decline.'

'Great-uncle told me, Kapetán Panayís.'

'The son, however, was educated and is now the driving spirit of our high school. Just a moment, you almost made me forget. Why didn't you tell me or your mother that they've thrown you out of high school for not paying the fees? He told me so himself; he says we owe them two pounds ... '

'I didn't want to upset her; we'll see what happens after the holidays.'

He realized that I was right and changed the subject.

'As soon as we get there, we'll set the deep-water lines down in the sea off Pig Island reef. Then we'll go inshore and we'll work the shallow-water line all night long; we'll set it and haul it again and again. Put the engine on full throttle, I want us to be at Pig Island before the sun goes down. The landmarks that my uncle, Kapetán Panayís, gave me can only be seen during the day and tonight there's no moon.'

We passed Cape Pachíammos, leaving the high shoreline with its dark seaworn rocks behind us and moving on to the bays with their fine light golden sand separated by low headlands. As we advanced, the rocks built up again until eventually the sandy beaches disappeared. We passed the second and then the third low hill. The shoreline rose again: we would be there in half an hour at the most; the *Argo* was making good progress, its bottom was clean and free of weeds.

She was a fine handsome vessel, six metres long, made in Syros, with a frame and beams of Samian pine. She had been ordered by his uncle, Kapetán Panayís, I think, and had used to belong to him. She had a transom stern[42] like that of a schooner – the type known as *skambavía* – with a perforated floor and a carved tiller. She stood up well to the sea, with a good draught and a good bottom. She wasn't covered with a deck; she was open with benches and seats around the stern, one in the middle next to the cover of the petrol engine, and one further forward behind the foredeck with a hole for the mast. Right up front, behind the bow stem, was the *fournos*, a special round opening big enough for a man to stand in when hauling in the fishing gear. For mooring it had ringbolts high up on the bow and on the stern.

A lot of people advised him to pull the seats out and fit the boat with a deck, to cover it over like all fishing boats. 'But she's a work of art and I'm not going to spoil her!' he would retort.

She was the most outstanding relic of the good old days: once he had kept her merely for his own pleasure and taken pride in her. At that time she had a sail, a lateen, with a short mast and a boom.[43] The mast was always fixed in position, rigged with its ropes, just behind the seat in the bow, with the sail furled on the boom hanging down at the side, and the rope fed through a point high up on the mast. Just one tug was needed to raise the boom. He christened her *Argo*; she was brilliant white all over, even the mast, the boom and the sail. The only thing that wasn't white was the blue cord beneath the gunwale.

At the *Kataklysmós*[44] festival he never once lost the race for fishing boats with lateen sails. With his uncle, Kapetán Panayís, at the helm, he always used to enter the harbour first with his sail billowing proudly ... and the others would follow behind. As soon as they crossed the finishing-line, he would slacken the sail-sheet,[45] run onto the bow, nimbly furl up the sail and pick up a large triton.[46] He would blow it three times and it would echo around the harbour. Just as he did then, now too he treated her like the apple of his eye, caring for her more than anything else.

He wouldn't let anybody touch her. Only his uncle, Kapetán Panayís, would board her, if the mood took him: he would undo the thin mooring ropes and turn her bow towards the harbour mouth. He would raise the boom high up onto the mast, open the sail, haul on the sail-sheet at the stern and take up the tiller.

He wouldn't let the sail fill out very much: he would nimbly tighten it by tugging the sail-sheet, for the *maïstros* would blow directly onto the sail. He would always skim past the lighthouse as was proper and then sail close to the *maïstros*. He would pass by Archangel's Rock,[47] which old timers used to say had once been thrown by the Archangel to sink the pirate ships that threatened the town. After Snake Island he would really open up and disappear on the open sea.

He would never take anybody with him. Only twice did he do me the favour of taking me with him and on both occasions I only heard him speak once we were back in the harbour. He liked to go out on his own and pit his wits against the weather he loved; he would remember the old *maïstros* routes, the days of the tall masts, the faded sails, the jibs, the lateens and the mainsails. He knew how to sail close to the wind and even upwind by tacking to and fro in a zig-zag course. He would sail against the *tramountána* and then later against the *garbís* lots of times, over and over again. 'Nobody really understands ... only those who have sailed in the Aegean, nobody else,' he would often say.

He had to lose sight of the island, to get far away from its shores. He enjoyed the open sea: the weather, the waters and the currents all knew him well and he talked to them for hours on end. Once they'd run out of things to say, he would suddenly push the tiller sideways, slacken the sail-line and let the sail billow out ahead like a balloon.

He would sail like this before the wind, sometimes at an angle to it, towards Snake Island, which he would now skim past, and a little later he would furl the sail and row into a small natural harbour with two or three metres of coarse sand at its innermost point. He would get out and stoop down nearby to drink the water from the spring that issued from the rock, and then go up to the church of the Glykiotissa. After paying his respects, he would return to the boat, take up the oars, row out of the cove and unfurl the sail again, making for the lighthouse, which again he passed within a whisker of and then entered the harbour. If ever the *maïstros* grew really rough or abated, nobody would go out to look for him; they knew he would return.

# 4

# Setting the Lines

I WAS SITTING IN THE STERN with the tiller under my arm but my thoughts, no longer occupied by the past, wandered elsewhere and began to dwell on other things ... on my friends who, in this fine weather, would no doubt be strolling along the pier behind the girls and flirting with them. Tomorrow I wouldn't be going to St Hilarion either for soccer practice or ... No, I wouldn't be doing any of those things as long as the fair weather lasted.

He baited the second deep-water line as well. He stood up, put it down on the floor of the bow and fetched the cuttlefish. He took the small Lapithos knife, which was always well honed, out of his pocket and began to cut the whitened flesh into strips and then into very small thin pieces. He fetched the long-line for shallow water and began to bait it. It consisted of a thin monofilament line, also laid carefully and methodically in a shallow round cane basket, with branch-lines tied to it about every five metres or so. One by one he took the small hooks out of the cork – about two hundred in all – and attached bait to them. Thin hooks were a nuisance, he would say, you had to handle them with care.

He had just finished when Pig Island appeared, a dark reef out in the open sea, a mile away from the mainland. I turned the bow towards it: it was true, the rock really did look like a pig; from a distance you could make out its snout, its back and its ears; only the legs weren't visible – they must have been under the water.

'We must get ready, the sun will go down soon ... head out to sea,' he told me as soon as I had brought the boat near Pig Island.

He stooped down beneath the foredeck and took out three buoy-lines laid in cane stools[48] that served as buoys, with their weights placed on top of them. Then he fetched two hurricane lamps, which he called *fanaria*, and lit them.

'This big stool with the big weight is for the sounding-line:[49] remember, every ten fathoms there is a knot, and you have to measure the depth quickly, but make sure you don't miss a knot ... Take her out a good way, line Pig Island up with the carob sheds – can you see them, on the shore directly below the road that leads up to the village of Chartzia?'[50]

'Don't we need any other landmarks?' I asked after I had brought them into line.

'No, the other thing we have to watch out for is the depth, fifty fathoms,' he said, taking over the tiller. 'Go up onto the bow and let out the sounding-line when I tell you to.'

He headed the boat out into the open sea, taking care to align the stern with Pig Island and the sheds. Suddenly he stopped and put the engine into reverse, and the boat came to a standstill.

'Okay, let her go!' he shouted.

I threw the lead weight of the sounding-line into the sea, letting the line slip through my palm. After I had counted four knots, I felt the line grow slack; it had reached the bottom. I hauled it up, counting the fathoms with outstretched hands, until I had reached the fourth knot.

'Forty-five fathoms,' I said as I continued to haul up the line.

'I'll take her out a little bit further,' he said, and he took the buoy-line out of a stool and tied a hurricane lamp inside it. 'We're quite far out; let's put lights on the two ends of the line so that we can find them easily and haul them in before it gets light, because after that it'll all get eaten by the seal. You might see it in the morning; the Pezounokremmoí[51] caves aren't very far away, that's its permanent home.' He stopped once again. 'Right, take a sounding.'

I cast the sounding-line back into the water and it reached the bottom half a fathom before the fifth knot. 'Fifty,' I shouted, and I began to haul it back up.

'Stop for a moment: tie the buoy-line to the stool and put it in the water. Watch the current.'

'There's no current at all,' I replied a few moments later, as I watched the line go straight down and become refracted in the calm water together with the light. 'Shall I switch off the engine so that we can set the lines as we row?' I asked as I hauled in the sounding-line.

'No, I'll set them with the engine on; we're behind time. Bring me a long-line ... ' He crossed himself. 'O Lord, show thy mighty power,' he said, then he bent down, carefully placed the cane stool with the lamp in the water and began to set the buoy-line as he opened up the engine.

As I laid the deep-water line on the seat at the stern, I couldn't help smiling to myself: in the morning, as soon as the line got caught up on the seabed, he would begin to curse and blaspheme wildly ... He noticed that I was smiling, turned round and gave me a fierce look.

When he'd finished setting the buoy-line, he tied the end of the long-line to its weight, turned the bow north-eastwards and began to set the long-line, with the engine at full throttle. The thick monofilament of the main line[52] slid through his palm and whenever a branch-line came up he opened his palm mechanically to let it pass through. One after the other, the short branch-lines with their big hooks that were attached to the thick monofilament of the main line whisked over the stern into the sea, sank and spread out on the seabed at intervals of about ten metres. All of the hooks were baited with fresh fragrant picarel: any fish passing by would pick up the scent, take a fancy to it and swallow it along with the hook. I looked on in amazement: few men could set a line like that, at full speed, handling the engine and the tiller at the same time. He glanced constantly back at the mainland. It was clear that he had other landmarks which he lined up with each other in order to follow the correct course, in order to keep exactly over the fishing bank so that the hooks would fall onto it and not in the muddy wastes at either side.

'It's a fishing bank for bottom long-lines,' he began to say, 'a great reef for big fish, for white groupers, stone bass and red bream. It's all coral rock, with clumps of plants here and there, but as narrow as the ridge of a mountain, with its sides dropping away to a depth of over a hundred fathoms. As we go on, it gets a bit deeper, down to about seventy fathoms, and then it drops suddenly and gets very deep and muddy. I hope we can get over it. Few, very few people know about it and I'm only just beginning to get familiar with it myself; Kapetán Panayís told me what signs to look out for. Tie the central buoy-line to the stool, at seventy fathoms, get ready.'

I picked up the other buoy-line and began to count from the weight onwards. When I had counted seventy fathoms, I tied the line to the stool and placed the line back inside it with its weight on top.

'Come on, take a sounding!' he shouted as he put the engine into reverse and stopped. There were five or six hooks left in the basket.

I threw the sinker[53] of the sounding-line into the water, counted six knots and immediately afterwards felt it touch the bottom.

'Sixty-two,' I replied and straightaway I swiftly hauled the line back up.

I handed him the sinker of the buoy-line that I had prepared for the middle section and he tied the end of the long-line to it. I lifted up the empty basket and put down the other one in its place. He tied the end of this new long-line to the same sinker, thus joining the two long-lines together, started up the engine and began to set the line again. I let the buoy-line run through my palm and when I felt it touch the bottom I threw the stool into the water.

'Can you see the *Astero*?' he asked me. 'They're anchored over in the shallows. They've set their nets; once we've finished we can go over to them.'

The sun was close to setting behind Pentadaktylos when the last hook went over – three hundred in all. He took the sinker of the sounding-line, tied the end of the long-line to it and let it sink slowly, measuring the depth at the same time. When it reached the bottom he tied another lamp inside a stool, placed it carefully in the water and stopped to watch it for a short while.

'There's no current at all. The crafty old girl is dead calm both above and below the surface,' he said, lighting up a cigarette. 'We've gone a bit over seventy fathoms. Never mind. We've hit a good spot, that's for sure. The lines have reached the bottom; when there is no current like this they go straight down. All the hooks must have gone down; they must have settled on the reef. The lines have spread out well too: you can just see our first lamp – the ends of the long-lines must be two miles apart. Take her up to our buoy-lamps so that we can check.'

I took her back towards our first lamp, towards the south-west. Everything was deep red: the peaks shaped like an upraised palm, the whole mountain, the sea, the sky – everything was enveloped in flames as if it had caught fire. There was no horizon: the sea and the sky had fused together.

'Don't worry, it wasn't us who caused this fire. Now take her over to where my brothers are.'

My uncles had set their nets and had anchored in a cove, near the half-ruined carob sheds. I drew the boat alongside them and we moored ourselves to them. My old man switched off the engine. He lifted up a plank in the floor of the stern.

'She's let in a lot of water, I wonder why? ... Get the *touloúmba* and empty it out,' he told me. *Touloúmba* was his word for the pump, which he had made himself with a pipe.

'It's a boat that's been out to sea, so what did you expect it to produce ... wine? Her timbers will be swollen by tomorrow,' Savvas remarked.

'Get your grub and come over here and eat with us ... You went out a long way, didn't you? How many fathoms down did you set the lines?' asked Charalámbis.

'We began at fifty, just as Kapetán Panayís told me,' he replied. Then he went on: 'I know the sea is calm and there's no current but it's still perishing cold ... it's really humid, isn't it!'

'Humidity is a sign of fine weather, you should be glad,' Savvas' voice rang out again.

I jumped into the *Astero*, which next to our boat looked like a caique, two metres bigger. My old man also got in, bringing everything my ma had prepared with him: bread, olives, onions, boiled potatoes and a bottle of wine. I sat between the three giants: they were an awesome sight. You could hear their great jaws working as they chomped away in silence. When a man eats he should keep quiet for he is in the presence of Jesus Christ, they would say. It was the same story at home. Nobody could speak at table until everyone had finished eating. I wanted to acquire a physique like theirs, but my body didn't seem to have made up its mind yet whether it was going to adopt my mother's Lapithiote frame or the build of these harbour folk here.

I ate quickly and returned to our boat, got the *touloúmba* and began to pump out the water. The cackle of a partridge briefly broke the infinite stillness and immediately afterwards a gentle breeze began to blow down from the mountain, ruffling the mirrorlike surface of the sea and filling it with ripples. With it descended the scent of the mountain, and the sea smelt sweetly of thyme.

'I see you've set all the nets,' my old man remarked on leaving the *Astero*.

'Yes, in about an hour's time we're going to haul them up and take out the fish. Then we'll reset the nets and hit the sack,' explained Charalámbis. 'When the sun comes up we'll haul them in again and head back for the harbour. That way we make two catches.'

'Why don't you make just one big catch in the morning? Once they're caught, fish don't get away,' I ventured to ask.

'That's enough from you ... you should learn to listen without speaking,' Charalámbis cut me short with a fierce look. 'You should also learn to respect the sea. A fisherman never leaves his nets set for longer than he has to. If the evening catch is left in the water by morning it will stink and it'll be eaten by rag worms, which is a crying shame ... '

'About an hour before sunset fish in deep waters begin to move towards the land, into shallower waters,' explained my uncle Savvas, who appeared to have taken pity on me. 'They continue to graze for about an hour even after the sun has gone down. That's the time you catch whatever you're going to catch in the nets. After that there's nothing. In the morning, again about an hour before sunrise they begin to go back to the deep waters, where they started from. If there are nets in their way, they'll get caught again, d'you get it?' he asked me patiently.

'We're going to work with the shallow-water line all night long; we're going to keep setting it and hauling it in, for as long as this sailor here can hold out,' my old man said, giving me a stern look.

'Stay close to the shore and keep your oars well away, not over our nets, d'you understand? And make sure you haul in the deep-water lines you've set out at sea before it gets light, otherwise the old bitch won't leave you anything,' yelled Savvas as we drew away from them.

'What's the old bitch?' I asked.

'The seal,' replied my old man.

# 5

# The Big Catch

It was well and truly dark when we found ourselves beneath the Pezounokremmoí, whose rocks soared straight up out of the water for about twenty metres. High up they were a reddish pink, gnarled by the wind and pitted with thousands of holes. Low down at water level they were jet-black and eroded by the sea, with hollows and deep caves. The heights were full of wild pigeons, and during the stillness of the night the females could be heard cooing. I looked around to see if I could catch a glimpse of the seal.

'Take her over there, where the cliffs begin.'

By the time we got there, he had fetched two stools and placed lamps inside them, tying their buoy-lines for a depth of five fathoms.

'We'll set it in shallow water, four fathoms deep at the most, so you don't have to take a sounding,' he said.

He hung one stool with its lamp on the forked stick on the stern, which before becoming a forked stick had once been a leafy branch on a tree. The dim light from the lamp gave the cliffs a grotesque appearance.

'Go inshore, switch off the engine and take up the oars. If you work, you won't get cold and you won't feel sleepy,' he told me, and as he placed the other stool in the water, he crossed himself and began to set the shallow-water long-line.

Working the oars, I followed the shoreline in silence. Sure enough, I began to feel warm. Within half an hour the line had been set. He took the stool with its lamp down from the fork and placed it in the water, after tying the end of the long-line to the sinker on the buoy-line. He lit up another cigarette. Half of it disappeared in his first drag.

'Start up the engine, let's go back slowly to our first lamp. Just make sure you don't cross over the line, take her well out.'

When we reached it, he turned off the engine, went to the bow and got into the *fournos*. Before I took up the oars, he asked me to hand him the empty basket and some bait that had already been cut up. He placed the basket at his side and stuck his knife into its rim, then laid out the bait on the edge of the gunwale.

'Show thy mighty power, O Lord ... ' he said to himself.

He crossed himself, bent down, lifted the stool out of the water and hung it on the fork. Then he turned up the flame a little.

'Let's see,' he said. 'There are stretches of sand here and there, so we're bound to pick up a weaver fish. I dread its poison.'

Gradually he began to haul in the long-line, laying it out in the basket and carefully hanging the small hooks on the cork, one after the other. Wherever bait was missing, he put a new piece on so that it would be ready for the next time he set the line.

'Come closer, row forwards, there's a fish coming up; I can feel it wriggling ... it's tugging ... fetch a basket for me to put the fish in ... put it between us on the floor ... move her away from the line a little bit ... hold it there ... whoa, go back ... '

He bent down and lifted up a white bream ... 'Show thy mighty power, O Lord,' he repeated, unhooking the fish and tossing it into the basket. He rebaited the hook with a piece of cuttlefish.

'Row forwards and go out further ... there are more coming up ... whoa ... go back, there's another one coming out of the water.'

He unhooked it, then another one and then another, six in a row. Then followed a few hooks without anything, just the gleaming white bait.

'Row forwards, quickly ... closer, come closer,' he began to shout. 'There's a big fish and it's pulling hard; the line's only thin ... it'll snap it and get away ... fetch the scoop-net ... row harder ... whoa, back! ... '

He took the scoop-net from me, bent down over the water and lifted out a huge dentex, which, as it lay enmeshed in the net, glistened like gold in the lamplight. He made no attempt to remove the hook but simply cut the branch-line and handed me the net. I looked at the fish in wonder: it wriggled as I took it out of the net, and then it lay on the floor of the boat vigorously beating its tail. It must have weighed five okas.[54]

'Hey, are you asleep? Row hard forwards.'

'I'm wetting the strops[55] of the oars to soften the rope.'

'D'you have to do that now? ... Come on, row forwards harder ... there's another one ... come closer ... the net.' He bent down, stretched out his arm, dipped the scoop-net into the water again and lifted out another golden fish, identical to the first.

'Hey, go back, you've gone over our nets,' echoed Charalámbis' voice from out to sea.

It must have been about two in the morning when he lit up a cigarette. 'Set the line ... haul it in ... row forwards ... row back ... come closer ... go out further ... ': with an endless string of shouts and oaths against God and the Panayia[56] we set and hauled in the line three times. He started up the engine, put out the lamps and sat at the tiller. I filled half a bag with the white bream, about twenty okas' worth, not counting the two dentex. I tidied up the shallow-water line and its buoy-lines at the back of the boat and then dug out two home-made woollen blankets wrapped in tarpaulins from the bow hold.

With the tiller under his arm, he continued to head out to sea, making a line for our two lamps, the closest of which was some four miles away. Above us, in the crystal-clear sky, the countless stars shone like glowing embers. The boat's wake, where the propellor had churned up the calm water, glistened in the starlight, forming a gleaming trail behind us. We drew near and the dark outline of Pig Island appeared. He went up close, very close and cast the grapnel anchor.[57]

'You sit down too, wrap yourself up in the blanket and the tarpaulin, have a rest. But don't fall asleep, you'll freeze. We'll rest for about an hour and then, with God's help, we'll haul in the deep-water lines before it gets light. Remember, we mustn't let the seal get there first. You heard what your uncle said.' I didn't answer. He went on: 'Don't be put off, praise God, we've had a good time.'

It was about four o'clock when he woke me up with the sound of the engine. My body was stiff with cold. He had raised the anchor and got the boat going. My breath was steaming, my nose had begun to freeze and I could only just feel my ears. The breeze stopped blowing off the land and the sea turned into a sheet of glass once more. In the distance the two lamps on our buoy-lines looked as if they were suspended from the sky, which on the previous evening had merged into the sea. The smallest stars had begun to fade; it wouldn't be long before the sun came up ... We were behind time; it looked as if he had fallen asleep as well. We drew near the lamp on the first buoy-line, the one we had set at fifty fathoms. He switched off the engine.

'Get rowing ... come closer so that I can pick up the stool ... I want you to be ready, always over the line, d'you understand? It's deep here and the reef has jagged edges ... If the line gets caught down there, we've had it ... and if it doesn't pull free, we'll lose both the line and the fish.'

He got into the *fournos*, remembered God again and crossed himself, murmured something and lifted up the stool. He untied the lamp, hung it next to the fork, and began to haul up the buoy-line, looping the line around his hand.

'Row hard backwards ... back and further out,' he said, 'the sinker's come off the bottom ... it'll come up at any moment ... row forwards now.'

As soon as the sinker on the end of the buoy-line came out of the water, he put the line in the stool, took the end of the long-line in his mouth and untied the sinker. Meanwhile I placed the empty basket in front of him.

'Move the boat away from the line, move it well away, there are some fish coming up, big ones, they must be red bream.'

He felt the fish wriggling as he pulled; the main-line jerked more and more as it neared the surface. He placed three hooks in the basket and then brought in a red bream, about two okas in weight. He unhooked it and threw it down at my feet.

'These are what you call fish,' he said, 'it's a joy to feel them pulling when you haul them up from the deep; it's a joy to see them when they come out of the water.'

He bent over and watched the line as it came up, his hair brushing the water. He sat up, and in the dim light of the lamp I noticed that he was smiling – strange, he wasn't shouting.

'More are coming up, a row of fish and hooks ... row forwards gently ... come a bit closer.'

Four came up in a row, one after the other, and then about ten hooks with just bait. Then followed a big grouper, then another one, then the bream began again; the floor was filled with big fish. I had never seen him so calm before. All the time he kept saying, 'Row backwards ... row forwards ... come up close ... move further out ...' but he wasn't shouting, he was whispering as if he didn't want to be heard by the fish, which he kept unhooking and tossing into the boat, half alive.

'We're reaching the end of the first long-line,' he said. 'When the sinker comes up, I'll hand it to you and I want you to bring in the central buoy-line as fast as you can, d'you understand?'

'Okay,' I replied, 'Don't worry.'

Then the first signs of day began to appear in an atmosphere of absolute peace and tranquillity: not a sound could be heard and not a single thing stirred, not even the sea. The darkness gradually began to lift, a rosy hue appeared in the east, and the dark leaden mass of the mountain became faintly visible. From the mountainsides the crowing of the first cocks could be heard, and then lights appeared moving along the coast road in a westerly direction.

'It's the local bus. See, we're not alone in the world. There are other people, though they have cares of their own,' my old man informed me, as he stopped hauling in the line for a moment.

'That's odd, what's going on? It's coming up very easily ... it's been cut ... the bastard – a dogfish, I bet ... what a bloody waste of fish, what a waste!' he began to shout angrily.

'Let's go and pick it up from the other end; there's our lamp over there,' I said.

As soon as the sinker came out of the water, he untied the ends of the long-lines, handed it to me and pensively lit up a cigarette. I lifted up the long-line he'd hauled in, took it to the stern, put the empty basket in its place and then hauled in the central buoy-line with its stool. I began to move the fish to the stern so that I could have room to stand when he suddenly began to growl.

'Leave all that ... get hold of the oars ... did you hear? Quickly ... row hard, come on, row hard!'

I stopped and looked at him.

'Row forwards as hard as you can, the long-line is on the surface, loaded with fish ... row hard forwards ... come on, row hard ... wake up, dozy!'

'Why are you yelling like that? Those are fish which have been caught and burst; that's what's brought the line up to the surface,' I protested, and I added: 'Now you won't have to tire yourself out dragging them up from seventy fathoms down.'

'If a shark or a dogfish comes by, or that bitch of a seal ... you heard your uncle Savvas ... it'll tear them to pieces, can't you see, it's getting light? Now belt up and row hard forwards.'

In the calm water the fish glistened in the light of dawn, running in a line back to the buoy-lamp. First he brought up a stone bass and then a huge white grouper, weighing almost twenty okas. I moved it to the stern as it was, in the water. Although it was dead, I had a tough job lifting it up and bringing it into the boat. A balloon full of air protruded from its big gaping mouth.

'There, that's why the long-line came up to the surface: all fish have an air sac under their backbone which helps them go up and down in the water. If they get caught on a hook, this fills up with air before they die. Also, if you bring them up quickly from the bottom, again it fills with air, and of course if it doesn't burst, it breaks away from the spine and comes out like this,' he said, pointing to the large balloon that was sticking out of the grouper's mouth.

A row of red bream followed; large ones, weighing two or three okas each. Nearly all the hooks had fish on them. His hands worked mechanically: as soon as he brought a fish in, he would take the knife out of his mouth and cut the branch-line; then he would throw the fish down at my feet and place the long-line, any old how, in the basket. He didn't unhook them so as not to waste time. I was rowing as hard as I could. There was no need for him to shout at me again or tell me to row backwards or go closer. I could see the line of fish ahead of me. We were getting nearer and nearer the lamp.

At one point the fish disappeared from the surface and I noticed that his hands were working more slowly; he was now putting in more effort as he brought the long-line and the buoy-line sinker up from the seabed. I let go of the oars and gazed at the slice of sun that had appeared and was casting its rays further and further over the horizon, until they finally reached us. Day had dawned.

From the foothills the merry, raucous sound of a bell could be heard, clanging twice in succession. It rang out, and echoed, a few times and then once again there was absolute peace and quiet.

'Well, look who's here,' he said, pointing towards the mainland.

At the side of the boat, a brown seal with big whiskers was staring at us with its head out of the water, munching a red bream. It held it like a human being with hands. I got the impression it was laughing.

'You're welcome to it, my love,' he said to her. 'If she eats it up, you give her one too ... a small one, though, so she won't get fat.'

I waited for her to eat it up, then when she had finished I picked up a red bream, leaned over the side and dipped it into the water. Without submerging, she slowly swam over, with her head out of the water, came in close and snatched it out of my hand. 'That's how it is,' I thought, 'today they make a fuss of her and on other days, when they haven't caught anything, they think she's a real bitch.'

There was another, much bigger one at Ayios Fanourios three miles west of the harbour; I'd seen it many a time. It struck me that he must be the mate of this one here, but why should they live on their own and apart from each other?

He hauled up the buoy-line, placed it in the stool and lit up a cigarette. He remained in the *fournos* on the bow, gazing at the fish that had covered the floor, burying my legs up to my kneecaps. He lit up another cigarette and prepared to get out.

'Pinch me so I know I'm not dreaming ... Where can I step?' he said, looking at the fish. 'I've never made such a big catch before.'

I took the oars out of the oarlocks, pushed a few fish to one side, started up the engine and began to head for the harbour.

'Go inshore, over to where they are.'

I latched on ... it was his life's dream. His best ever catch. It was no longer something he dreamed about on stormy winter nights with a howling north wind. The big fish lay before him, filling his boat ... The men who had taught him must see them.

I turned our bow towards the *Astero*. His brothers had begun hauling in their nets, and the sun was now fully up. On the bow, Savvas was bringing the nets up out of the shallow water with ease. They were loaded with fish. Reddish mullets were tossing and writhing about, and there were occasional white flashes of other fish. Before I drew alongside, Charalámbis, who was pulling on an oar, asked, 'How did you get on? Why are you so quiet?'

'Pretty poor really,' said my old man as we drew alongside.

'Stone me, you lucky bastards ... you lucky bastards,' Charalámbis exclaimed as soon as he saw the fish. 'Did you catch them? I don't believe it ... Hey, Savvas, come and see what our young brother has got ... He's always been lucky, the big oaf.'

'Well I'll be bloody damned!' he replied, somewhat piqued.

He beckoned me to move off and just as we moved away from the *Astero* he called out to them.

'Would you like me to hang on so that I can tow you back to harbour?' he jested, tossing a red bream into the *Astero*.

'Well I'm blowed. Young Christakis is making fun of us,' said Savvas.

He came to the stern, lit another cigarette, put the tiller under his arm and headed the boat towards the harbour. I was shivering in the morning cold.

'Come here and sit by me,' he said, making room for me beside him. 'Together with the white bream and the dentex we must have between two hundred and two hundred and twenty okas of fish ... We'll celebrate Christmas like we used to ... when I used to invite everybody round on my name day ... do you remember? Are you thinking about your school fees? ... Let me tell you something ... nets are okay, you always catch fish ... not many, but you'll never go hungry ... it's a bit like having a regular job with a salary ... but long-lines ... We can pay off Kestas as well, we've driven the poor bloke crazy over the credit he's given us; he's only a grocer, not a millionaire.'

He smoked and talked incessantly. At some point I lost track of what he was saying and felt myself being wrapped in the blanket.

# 6

# Boatbuilding

I woke up as we entered the harbour. All the boats were in; they had set their nets or lines nearby, around the harbour. Only the *Astero* was missing. No sooner had we drawn alongside the quay and tied the boat loosely to the quayside steps than the local riffraff came up, their numbers swollen by reinforcements and the small fry of the harbour who admired them. They ran up in order to … 'inspect the ship',[58] as they would say, and to have a laugh as usual. When they drew near, however, they didn't say a word: there was no banter, no jokes; they just looked at each other.

'You buggers are all very quiet today,' my father remarked. 'Have any of you seen Kiámilos[59] the fishmonger?'

'There he is; he's on his way,' one of them replied, and then, to break the silence, he asked, 'Where did you catch the fish, Christaki?'

'Below St Hilarion,' he replied, and then he called out, 'Hey, make way, let the man through.'

He had noticed the fishmonger's head standing out above theirs some distance away; he was a tall fellow. They made way for him and he passed through, went down the steps and paused for a while, eyeing the fish thoughtfully. Then he said, 'We've got a problem; everybody's had a good catch. What's more, Kyrenia can't eat all this fish just now, there's too much of it, they're expensive fish, it's winter and all the restaurants are closed, it's almost Christmas … I'll take the white grouper and the three other big groupers to Katsellis' hotel,[60] he always takes the big ones … and I might just sell ten okas of red bream as well … I think you'll have to ring Lefkosia and get your friend Mitros to come and take the rest.'

'Take whatever you want, whatever you think you need,' my old man replied gloomily.

He slowly got out of the boat, went up the short flight of steps and headed for the Customs House.

'I'm going to phone Mitros,' he called out to me.

I stayed behind to help the fishmonger, who was picking out the big groupers and the white groupers. We got the fish out of the boat and then I gave him five red bream, as he had asked for. He hung them all on his bicycle.

My old man returned a short while later purple with rage, angrier than he'd ever been before. The riffraff stood back, scattering in alarm.

'Who needs friends like that!' he cried. 'There are too many ... it's holiday time ... who will eat them? ... He'll take them but for only three shillings an oka ... Who needs friends like that? ... No, I'm not going to let him have them, I'll chuck them back into the sea.'

He got into the boat and sat down, lighting up one cigarette after another, gazing constantly at the fish. Suddenly he sprang up.

'Hang on, I'll be back,' he said. He hurriedly got out of the boat, climbed up the steps to Trypití and vanished.

Not long afterwards the Lefkosia bus drew up by the steps above the boat. He got off, carrying five tall round cane baskets. We put the fish into them and then he lifted them onto the bus's luggage rack,[61] with the aid of the local riffraff. As he tied the baskets in place, he hurriedly began to list the things I should do.

'I'm going to Lefkosia, to sell them one by one; I know where to go. I've already rung your mother's brothers; they've got a grocer's store in Ledras Street and they're going to let their customers know. In the meantime, you clean and tie the boat up properly ... take the one grouper I've left to my uncle, Kapetán Panayís, and give the other one to Kakkápetris. Then go home, have a rest and at midday come down here, and bring food, petrol and oil for the lamps. Tidy up and get the long-lines ready; we'll go out again as soon as I get back. We'll tie on the hooks I cut off and add the bait on the way there ... leave only the two deep-water long-lines in the boat.'

He boarded the bus and then got off again, hurried up to me and said in a low voice, almost in my ear, 'Make sure you don't breathe a word; I don't want anyone finding out where we caught the fish ... d'you understand?'

The sun was high overhead when I went down to the harbour, which had really come to life after the calm weather of the previous day. It was another warm day, without a cloud in the sky or the slightest breeze, and the sea, like the day before, looked as if it had set firm, like a sheet of glass. The *Astero* had returned and was tied up in its usual place and the fishermen were all there, gathering in the nets that had been spread out, rebaiting the long-lines and winding the buoy-lines back into their stools. Everything had to be ready for that night and the day was short, the shortest in the year. Some were preparing to lay their nets that evening, to make two catches. I saw the fishmonger approaching: he called out to me and I went over to him.

'Seven pounds for the thirty-five okas of groupers that Katsellis took and three for the ten okas of red bream,' he said, counting out the money for me. 'Tell your old man exactly what I've just told you.'

I took the money and went down the steps to get into the boat. The riffraff knocking about the harbour rushed over and came and stood above me, on the steps. They had noticed a couple of individuals sidling up to me and ran over to lend me some support.

'Where did you catch the fish?' I heard someone ask.

I raised my head and saw Kemalis and Bekiris.[62] They had noticed from over the way that I was alone and thought it was a good opportunity.

'Below St Hilarion,' I replied.

'Aren't you ashamed of yourself, sonny? You're having us on ... We saw you; you were on your way back from further out.'

They hadn't thought much of my reply, but it went down well

with the gallery assembled behind them, who began to poke fun at them.

Suddenly the harbour erupted: whistles and cries echoed all round, and everyone came out of the coffee-houses. On the road by the Customs House old Chatzifotís[63] appeared, with, as always, a basket in one hand and a stick in the other. At the sound of the first whistles he began to curse and threaten everybody, brandishing his stick.

Charalámbis, who was gathering in the nets spread out on the flat piece of ground beneath the steps of the ruined tower, could not tolerate this injustice, had never been able to bear it, and flew into a rage. He felt sorry for the old man because he was the only person in the whole town that did up the flat roofs every year before winter set in; it was he who laid out and pounded the dark *karmióhoma*,[64] making it like cement so that the roofs would not leak as soon as it rained.

'Shut up, you bastards; shame on you! ... Damn you all!' he shouted angrily.

His voice resounded like a bell around the harbour, reducing everyone to silence even before the old man had vanished into Trypití. Nobody dared to answer back or whistle again. They feared him as a man and respected the proud seaman, knowing full well that he was not a man of idle words. In the carob season he gave everyone a good day's wages. It was he and his lighters that loaded the carobs onto the ships, and they found steady work for two whole months, never mind what the merchants said. The most important thing, though, was that he brought back, even for only a short while, something of the old days.

At one point, about ten years earlier, he had realized that the last thing left in the harbour, the work with the carobs, was not going at all well, and was also on its way out like everything else. He saw that loading was a slow, time-consuming business, and the shipowners and dealers grumbled because the lighters that sailed in and out of the harbour to the ships were very slow. Very often loading would stop as soon as the weather got a little bit worse, even when there was no wind.

In order to avoid the worst, he had sold the last piece of land that he owned, called in Mastro-Panáos, who had been lured away to Famagusta, and asked him to build him a big boat with an engine that could tow the lighters in order to speed up the loading. Tears had filled the old craftsman's eyes: he was getting on in years and he'd missed the beautiful harbour and the harbour folk, even if he hadn't been born there.

He had been forcibly uprooted many times before he first settled here. He could just about remember how, as a little boy, he had left Antalya along with many others, and was forced by some soldiers to tramp in the cold and the heat for a whole year. Only he, and no other member of his family, had reached Smyrna alive. The boat-builders had taken pity on the weak and lonely little boy, picked him up, taught him a trade and turned him into a craftsman. After that he was uprooted and ruined again on several other occasions, until he eventually came to our beautiful port. He developed a deep love for it as everything was like what he had known in his childhood: the gardens of the houses, the mountains, the trees, the sea. He thought that he had finally come to rest, that he had made himself a safe and permanent anchorage at Tsiakkilerí. Yet need drove him out of there as well, though for the first time he was not forced to leave by violent means. With a broken heart he scraped out a living of a sort in Famagusta, which had by then become a big port.

As soon as he received the message, he hastened back to the small port, to be reunited with dear old friends, to eat and drink with them, and to build boats again, even though there were no boatyards at Tsiakkilerí. He brought all his tools with him: his two adzes, his chisel, his hole saw, his other hand-saws, his drill with its string, his wooden mallet with its caulking gear, and his cross-cut saw – all hand tools. When he arrived he said that he would build it in the harbour, high up on the road beneath the half-ruined ancient arches, which had once also been a boatyard; thousands of years before the ancients had built their own vessels there.

He immediately took on all the responsibilities and problems of the task in hand, carefully studying in his mind the length, width and draught that were required, as well as the type of bow and stern. The plans were all drawn up in his mind, ready for execution. It had to be a strong boat, with a strong frame made of tough wood because those blasted engines were no joke; they made the hull shudder.

He went round the orchards and found the black mulberry trees that he wanted: thick ones with arching boughs and curves for the ribs. He cut them down and carted them off to the harbour. Two men in baggy breeches – one in black and the other, Kemalis, in white ones – set to work and began to pull on the cross-cut saw with its thick teeth, tearing through the tough sweeping boughs in order to turn them into broad wooden beams.

The master boatbuilder set up the keel, after managing to find the squared timbers from Asia Minor that he wanted. He asked for a cockerel, a large one with a bushy tail. He placed it on the keel and, holding it down by its legs, struck off its head with one swing of his adze. He let all the blood run out onto the keel. So it had to be: a sacrifice had to be made in order to grant the boat a long life on the waves.

He applied all his skill to the construction of the bow-stem, the part of the boat that would cleave through the waves. He fashioned the special toothed joint and fitted the stem firmly into the keel. At the other end of the keel he fixed the stern-post into position and began to cut the ribs with their strange curves and fix them onto the keel in a row, each one span away from the next, beginning in the middle. His two adzes – one broad-headed and the other narrow, one in his hand and the other on his shoulder – worked incessantly, doing almost all of the work. He wanted to build a transom stern and put the propellor deep down as the boat had to be able to tow, to haul well.

When he had finished constructing the ribs, he fixed short thick wooden beams that he called *stragaliés* in between them. He fashioned and matched up the two thick supports for the engine, which for months had been waiting outside, and began to plank the shell. Later he made some benches and the floors, covered the boat with a deck and fixed two strong tow-bars in position at the back on the stern which were needed for towing the lighters.

When the boat was ready – caulked and painted white, with the engine and its tall funnel in the middle – the harbour folk gathered around it together with the local riffraff and children and other onlookers. The Trypití terrace high above the harbour filled with people, as did the other terrace further over to the left, the steps of the half-sunken ruined tower. Everyone wanted to help but Mastro-Panáos, who was directing operations with his adze still on his shoulder, turned them away, recruiting just a few, as many as he needed for the task. He was very fond of them all, despite the fact that for over eight months they had pestered him a great deal, especially the local riffraff. The old man had laughed and joked along with them but there were times when he'd got upset; he hadn't been able to take any more and he'd thrown his adze at them.

They smeared the wooden slippers beneath the keel with sheep's grease and began to push it slowly, sliding it inch by inch towards the quay below the castle where the rocks were lower and it would be easier to push it down to the sand.

Dressed in his best clothes, Charalámbis stood at the water's edge next to the old craftsman. Together they admired the boat, which looked big, impressive and beautiful. Suddenly, as soon as it entered the water, about ten people ran up, lifted Charalámbis high up into the air and threw him into the water. So it had to be: that was the custom. 'Good luck and long may you sail in her, Kapetán Charalámbis!' they cried, and the crowd went wild with enthusiasm.

From that moment on the *Astero*, as she was christened, became the first engine-powered vessel in the north and the queen of the harbour. For ten years now, every April and May, for two whole months, she had ceaselessly towed the loaded lighters, taking them out to the ship that would lie anchored outside the harbour.

The work with the carobs continued, it didn't die out; something of the old days remained. Mastro-Panáos forgot himself and never left again; he stayed, even though he was eventually forced to make barrels ... and clogs ... He endured the shame so that he could spend the rest of his life in the beautiful port, and he did stay.

# 7

# Harbour Matters

I GOT INTO THE BOAT loaded with everything he had ordered. I cleaned, thoroughly washed and tidied up the boat, removed the small amount of water that she had taken in, tidied up the two long buoy-lines and the sounding-line and filled the pitcher with cool water from the tap nearby. Then I sat down to tidy up the long-lines, beginning with the one whose hooks had been cut off – almost half of them were missing. The discarded hooks were in the basket among the pieces of fishing-yarn that were tangled up with the long-line. I fetched an empty basket, picked up the end of the long-line and began to transfer it into the empty basket. Whenever a branch-line came up I pinned the hook onto the cork around the rim. I tied a new hook onto all those that lacked one. I noticed that the branch-lines were shorter ... they should have been changed as well but I hoped that he would like them as they were and not kick up a fuss.

Suddenly the boat jolted: Karmiotis, a manic long-line fisherman, had pulled it and got in, and after sitting himself down next to me offered to help me tidy up the long-line. He's after something, I thought: I bet he wants to find out exactly where, on which bank we caught the fish. The local riffraff caught sight of him and all ran up to see what was going on.

No sooner had he sat down than, in a hushed voice as sweet as sugar, he asked, 'Tell me, young Christaki, where did you set your lines yesterday?'

'Out at sea, opposite St Hilarion,' I replied in a loud voice so that the riffraff above could hear.

They began to jeer, even though they hadn't heard his question.

Pirillas immediately wrote in big letters on a piece of cardboard THE RED BREAM WERE CAUGHT AT AÏ-LARKOS ... THE GROUPERS ON PENTADAKTYLOS and he hung it on the forked stick at the stern. The harbour echoed with laughter. Karmiotis made a hurried departure with his tail between his legs. Surely nobody else would now dare to ask again.

They left me as soon as Pateras, the big octopus catcher, appeared. He was barefoot and had his trouser legs rolled up, even though it was December. In one hand he held his fish-spear like Poseidon and in the other his old basket, out of which, through a hole, dangled the leg of an octopus. One of the local riffraff tried to pull the octopus out by the dangling leg but he felt him do so and drove him off with his trident.

He halted on the steps when he saw me and simply greeted me, without asking any questions; he never asked, for he always respected fishermen's secrets. He himself never gave anything away, especially when it concerned octopus: he knew the weight and the den of each and every one of them down to a depth of six fathoms. He only fished for them by order, depending on what size the customer wanted. If they wanted a big one, he would go down to the sea and catch one; if the customer wanted a small one, he would refuse, for he never caught or killed small octopuses.

He did this kind of work all winter long, spearing octopus and sometimes fishing with a rod – rainbow wrasse in periods of calm and white bream in stormy weather. When spring arrived, on the first day of Holy Week he would begin going round the houses and selling the seaweed that he pulled out from shallow rocks, the sea dye known as *mallouppa*, so that housewives could dye their red eggs.

On Holy Saturday he would pile up all the tree trunks and pieces of wood that had been gathered together during Lent by the local children and enthusiasts and he would light the Easter *lambratziá*[65] beneath the church of the Archangel.

Once the *lambratziá* had died out, his main operations would begin. He would fill the sea, to the left and right of the harbour, from Snake Island as far as Karákoumi, with fish traps, large ones for groupers and smaller ones for parrot fish and salpa, all of a round flattish shape, with the mouth on top tapering inwards, and all made from the slender twigs of wild myrtle trees. He would select a different depth and patch of stony seabed for each trap, always in a hollow. First of all he would feed the fish, throwing down bait to encourage them to graze in that particular area. When he saw that the fish were taking the bait, he would lay his traps without ever setting up a buoy or a reed on the surface[66] as others did; he guarded his secrets. He knew the seabed well; every morning and afternoon he would pass over it in his small boat. He would look into his glass and find the traps straightaway; one by one he would haul them up onto the boat, remove the fish, place fresh bait inside, and then let them sink back down into the water, each to its own particular place.

This work lasted all summer long, with only one break during the two-day *Kataklysmós* festival. At that time, during the nautical contests in the harbour, he had another mission: he had to smear the Slippery Mast with grease, to scatter the apples to see who could find the one that was marked, and to release the duck for the swimmers to chase.

In November he would begin his studies of the octopus again. First of all he would go around to locate those which had hatched during the summer, to find out where they had set up their dens and how much they had grown. He would search for the empty shells that they left outside their holes ... the leftovers of their meals, which betrayed the location of their permanent dens ... he needed to know, like the weight of each of them individually.

'I see you're going out again ... well, hope you land a lot of fish and Happy Christmas!' he said and he began to move off.

Then old Vasílagas appeared; emerging from his *Naftikó Kentro*,[67] next to the half-sunken Koulas, he descended the steps, with his white apron fastened around his plump waist. The local riffraff followed him, without making a sound. They all knew what was going on: earlier they had managed to find a serious, respectable and reliable informer to feed him with the false information that a caique had appeared out to sea. The old man had grabbed his big nautical telescope and limped towards the lighthouse steps.

'What is it, uncle? Whose caique is that heading this way?' the riffraff behind him asked, straight-faced.

'There's a caique coming... it'll be Salisvourís's... they're bringing walnuts... the police'll be here... they'll be taking statements... they'll put 'em all in prison.'

They all pretended to believe him and followed the old refugee from Asia Minor high up onto the lighthouse mole, even though Salisvourís' caique lay opposite, abandoned for years beneath the castle after being smashed to pieces by a *tramountána*. Soon afterwards loud jeers rang out from the lighthouse and once again the harbour echoed with noise.

This harbour had a history; it tested one's nerves. If anyone dared to walk around it without keeping their wits about them, they would come a real cropper.

I had just finished tidying up the other long-line when my old man suddenly emerged from Trypití, walking hurriedly and holding a bag. It must contain bait, I thought. From a distance he looked tired, even though he was smiling. I untied the boat and pulled her against the quayside. He came down the steps, got in and sat next to the engine cover, lighting up a cigarette. Then, after checking everything with a quick glance around, he beckoned me to start. I placed a long-line next to him, then started up the engine and got the boat going. We left the harbour.

'Did you give one grouper to Kapetán Panayís and the other one to Kakkápetris?' he asked.

'Yes, but why did you send Kakkápetris a fish? What do you owe him?'

'A lot, because before we go out fishing he's the only one that opens up and makes coffee for us without ever taking any money.'

'The old captain looked run-down to me; it looks like he's caught a cold. Just think, a day like this and he hasn't come down to the harbour. He says he wants to see me on New Year's Eve,' I said, changing the subject.

'Don't you worry, Kapetán Panayís has got a long time to go yet, he's in good health ... head towards Chrysokava; be careful, they're setting nets, keep your eyes skinned.'

Loukís, the fisherman from Lapithos, was setting his nets, standing upright in the stern of his boat with a smile on his face as always, with Psipshís helping him out on the oars. Further along, near Karákoumi, was Bekiris with his eldest son, Suleyman. He was a hard worker and a good fisherman, said my old man, but what else could he do, the poor bloke; he had ten mouths to feed – plus another two, if you included him as well.

'Going out for another big one?' Bekiris called out to us, as he continued to set his nets.

'The fishmonger gave me ten pounds: seven for the thirty-five okas of groupers and the rest for ten okas of red bream. That's exactly what he told me,' I said, and I gave him the money.

'That's four shillings an oka for the groupers and six for the bream,' he said to himself after a few moments' thought. 'Good for him, he knows what he's doing; he's helping us all out, keeping the prices up.'

He began to bait the long-line with the picarel that he had brought with him. A short while passed.

'You didn't ask me how I got on,' he said. Without waiting for a reply, he continued: 'I dropped into our place and gave your mother fifty-four pounds and a few shillings. I sold the fish to the folk in Lefkosia: eight shillings an oka for the red bream and the dentex, five for the groupers and the stone bass, and six for the white bream. There was real mayhem in the grocer's store in Ledra Street; I had no trouble at all, you saw how quickly I came back.'

I wondered just how big the catch had actually been: I knew that it would definitely have to be worked out at some stage.

'How many okas of fish did you take to Lefkosia?' I asked, albeit a little tardily.

'Are you any good at adding up? ... Ten okas of dentex, eighteen of white bream, eighty-five of red bream and forty-five okas of groupers and stone bass. How many okas do you make that?'

'One hundred and fifty-eight, plus the forty-five that Kiámilos took: two hundred and three okas,' I replied.

'Add to that another twenty odd that I gave away in various places ... Get the grub out, I'm hungry ... What has your mother packed for us?'

I unfolded the tablecloth; inside there was some bread, some olives, two spoons and a small earthenware pot full of *pourkoúri piláfi*.[68]

'Luxuries,' he said and he began to gulp down the pilaf as if it were soup. 'The weather is just as good as it was; we should get another good catch. As soon as we get there, we'll set both of the long-lines in the same place, then we'll have a kip until midnight. Then we'll haul them in and, with God's help, before it gets light we'll be back in the harbour. With a bit more help from God, we can even pay off that fucking debt on the house ... '

Suddenly two flying fish shot over the bow in alarm. They flew low, trailing their tails over the water. They flew out towards the open sea for about fifty metres and then plunged back in, each etching a line in the calm water.

Half an hour before the sun went down in the same spot, behind the same mountain, he crossed himself again, said 'Show thy mighty power, O Lord,' and began to set the same long-lines again with the engine at full throttle, over the same fishing-bank, in the same waters and in the same weather conditions – calm, with no breeze and no current.

From out at sea some gulls appeared, heading in our direction, although they were not diving or playing with the water but flying high as if in haste.

'It's just a coincidence,' he said, 'it can't be a sign of a change in the weather.'

He saw the gulls settle on the rocky outcrop of Pig Island and stopped setting the lines for a moment. He took a few long hard looks at the northern horizon and then began setting the lines again. The last hooks went down, he joined the end of the long-line to the sinker on the sounding-line, sounded the depth – seventy-two fathoms – fastened the lamp to the stool, bent over, placed it in the water and lit up a cigarette. He stayed there for a while, lost in thought, carefully studying the current and occasionally looking around, mostly towards the north.

'Again there's no current, the sly old fox isn't stirring, like yesterday ... take her behind Pig Island and cast anchor.'

By the time I had cast anchor and switched off the engine he had spread out a piece of tarpaulin on the floor of the bow, put on his *partesou*, wrapped himself in one of the blankets and fallen into a deep slumber. At once his loud snoring could be heard, and the gulls perched on Pig Island took fright, rose and flew off towards the mainland.

# 8

# The Shark

Shortly before midnight he woke me up. He folded up the blankets and stowed them away under the bow. He noticed that I was trembling, that my teeth were chattering from the cold and he picked up the bottle containing a small amount of wine.

'Go on, take a swig, it'll do you good; once you start rowing you'll warm up,' he said.

He picked up the crank and started up the engine. Then he raised the anchor, gathering the rope up in loops. He stowed these away as well in the space under the bow: it was amazing just how much would fit in there. I put the oars in the oarlocks and rowed away from Pig Island. A gentle breeze was wafting down from the mountain. I noticed that the boat's seats were dry; there was no moisture at all. He must have noticed it as well but hadn't said anything. I let go of the oars, took hold of the tiller and headed the boat towards our first lamp.

'Head for the other one, we'll start out in the deep water now that we're fresh; there's no current, so when we've finished we'll be two miles nearer the harbour.'

I turned the *Argo*'s bow towards the second lamp, the one lying further out, to the north-east. I put the engine on full throttle but realized that the boat was not making much headway; there was a strong current running against our bow. He sat thoughtfully, looking constantly out to sea; his eyes shone in the starlight, fixed on the northern horizon.

'Go past our lamp and switch off the engine,' he said in a barely audible voice.

When I had passed the lamp I switched off the engine and took up the oars. The square cane stool was leaning over on one side, half submerged, while a furrow of water could be clearly seen issuing from its base, winding around it and running away towards the west. The buoy-line appeared to be pulling on it from below, keeping it anchored in position. Fortunately the lamp was still alight, although the glass had become a little bit smudged.

'The current is like a river, it's going over there, in the opposite direction, towards the west ... row hard ... take her up to the lamp.'

We drifted about twenty metres away from the stool, then I turned the boat towards the west and began to row hard towards the lamp. He kept looking around anxiously, though always more urgently towards the north. Normally the current ran in an easterly direction, towards the *levante*. For seamen a strong current in the opposite direction was a sign of a change in the weather, a forewarning of a *tramountána*.

'The current itself will carry us, there's no need to row forwards ... in fact, row backwards, keep going backwards ... d'you understand?'

He crossed himself, uttered his prayer 'Show thy mighty power, O Lord,' bent down and took the stool out of the water. He took out the lamp, turned the flame up a little, hung it on the forked stick beside him and hastily began to pull up the buoy-line, gathering it up in loops, as he constantly scanned the northern horizon.

'Row hard backwards ... you've crossed over the long-line ... row backwards and bring her a bit closer ... We'll finish before the weather changes, don't worry. If a *tramountána* does come in, it'll come at dawn, just before it gets light. If we have to, we can go and take shelter in Limiónas, a little farther down ... it breaks the force of northerly gales.'

When the sinker came out of the water, I put it in the stool along with the buoy-line. I picked up the stool and placed an empty basket beside him. He began to haul in the long-line. He bent over the water and gazed into it, looking from side to side. In the lamplight I could see him smiling; for a moment he'd forgotten about the signs of a change in the weather. Now he was captivated by the sheer joy of the long-line; he could feel fish wriggling below, that was for sure.

'Row backwards ... go on, take her back ... a bit closer to the long-line,' he said, almost in a whisper, 'there's not just one, there are quite a few ... they must be red bream; I can tell from the way they tug on the line.'

He placed four or five hooks in the basket and then brought up the first fish, a deep red bream, and then another three in a row, big lively fish like those we'd caught the day before. One by one he unhooked them and tossed them onto the floor of the bow, where they writhed about beating their tails against the wood and against my feet.

'Shall I fetch the bag and put them in it? Yesterday they made my feet bleed.'

He didn't answer; his mind was on the fish below. The current, however, really was as strong as a river; suddenly the bow of the boat swung round towards the east and I had to keep rowing hard all the time against the strong current in order to stay in position.

'Row forwards and bring her right up close, the current's dragging us away ... come on, row hard, put your back into it,' he said. 'There are more coming up ... no, leave it, we don't need the bag ... now move her away ... that's it!'

He brought in another two bream and then suddenly gave a start: his movements changed and became more agitated; he swung from side to side, looking underneath the boat. He could feel something incredibly heavy ... it wasn't the line caught up anywhere or entangled on the seabed ... it was alive and extremely heavy.

'Row forwards,' he cried, 'the line's behind us ... it's something big ... row forwards and move her away ... move her well away.'

He pulled on the line with his strong arms, with all the strength he could muster, just like the fish beneath him: they were locked in a trial of strength. As he pulled, the thick yarn slipped through his hands, slicing into his fingers and palms and making them bleed, but he didn't give up.

'Row forwards ... row forwards as hard as you can ... row against the current ... row into it hard, heave ... heave ... heave.'

I rowed about ten powerful strokes. He stopped pulling for a few moments. He paused for breath and then, summoning up all his strength, pulled up the arm in which he was holding the long-line, gained about a metre and swiftly looped the main-line around the bow stem. He coiled it around the stem three or four times and then grasped the line in his left hand; there was no need for strength now. The strong transparent monofilament line, coiled around the wood, tautened and let off bubbles that glistened in the water.

'Now you can pull as hard as you like,' he said to the fish and then he turned towards me. 'Row hard forwards, into the current, and then quickly cut the hooks off the last few branch-lines so that we don't get caught by them if I have to slacken the line.'

After he had had a good rest, he wrapped a piece of tarpaulin that he had taken from the *fournos* around his right hand, bent over and in the same strong hand grasped the main-line, which led down into the water a metre away from the bow stem. He pulled it up hard, as high as he could, and then let it down for a few moments. He repeated this about thirty times until he realized that the fish was no longer pulling downwards. It now began to circle around the boat and gradually come up to the surface. Suddenly our bow veered round to the west, and I rowed backwards as hard as I could, over and over again. With one hand I quickly seized the grappling-hook and put it by my side – just in case I needed to use it, I thought.

'Well I'll be damned, it's a big dogfish, a shark; at first I thought it was a tunny. But where d'you think you're going, mate? I'm not going to let you off. I'm going to pull up on this end and you can pull down on yours but where's it going to get you? You'll either break or you'll snap the line and get away,' he explained to the fish. 'He must have swallowed the hook; it's gone right down into his belly, there's no other explanation. The device is designed for big fish but not for sharks,' he said to me, and then went on, 'pull hard on the oars, bring her up to the long-line; now that I'm going to start bringing him in, I want you to cut off every hook that comes in. You never know, the bastard might get his strength back and try and go down; be careful you don't cut the main-line.'

He unwound the line from the bow stem and began to haul it in. I cut off five hooks and chucked them into the sea. He brought it in close; its silhouette was just visible in the dim lamplight. As it circled round it looked enormous. I compared it with the boat: it was almost three metres long.

'A thresher, a thresher shark,' he said. 'Not a very big one, but he's incredibly strong. His tail fin is as long as his body. A rare sight in these waters. Sharks don't have an air sac like other fish, that's why dynamite doesn't kill them; they don't burst and they don't die easily. I've got to wear him down ... I'm being kind to him.'

He brought it in closer, I cut off another three hooks, and then he began to let it gradually move away, making sure that the line was always taut. Then he began to bring it in again, and it came in without putting up much resistance. Again he let it move away. Again he hauled in the line and brought it closer, with even less effort. I removed another two hooks.

'That's the only way you'll break,' he reminded it.

He slackened the line again. Then he brought the shark back in, very close this time, so that it brushed against the boat, and I cut off another three hooks. For a fourth time he let it move away, and this time it went down, towards the bottom, barely pulling on the line, carried down more by its own weight.

'We've got him. Cut off the big sinker, the one on the sounding-line,' he said, 'leave about a metre of line and put it next to me on the deck. Pick up the grappling-hook and get ready; when I bring him alongside stick the hook into his mouth and push against the gunwale to lift him out of the water – just a bit, only his head, d'you understand?'

'Yes, okay,' I said.

I rowed five or six powerful strokes, all against the current, cut the sinker off the sounding-line, placed it next to the basket and, as he had told me, picked up the grappling-hook and waited. He brought it in close; it put up no resistance at all. When it drew near the boat, I could see its teeth shining and the fishing-line coming out of the side of its mouth. Its huge tail was barely moving, slowly heaving from side to side. He brought it in even closer so that it was almost touching the bow, its mouth slowly opening and closing. He held the main-line for a short while in his left hand, while he wound the sounding-line around his strong right hand, with the sinker hanging about half a metre below it.

'Right, now!' he cried, and I thrust the grappling-hook quickly into its mouth, then pulled it back a bit and raised its head, using the gunwale as a lever. It began to writhe and shook me from head to toe. I summoned up all my strength and held firm while I watched him whirl the sinker around and bring it down as hard as he could on the shark's forehead. There was a loud crack and it stopped writhing. All I could feel now was the weight of its dead body.

'It's all yours,' he said and he came out of the *fournos*. 'Take it onto the stern.'

Without lifting it up, I dragged it back to the stern just as it was, lying at the side of the boat with the grappling-hook jammed into its mouth. My old man came over, made a noose with a thin piece of rope and passed it over its tail. He motioned to me and I raised the head with the grappling-hook, while he lifted the tail by pulling on the noose. When it was well clear of the water and both head and tail appeared above the gunwale, he grasped it by the middle with his other hand and pulled it in. It fell into the boat, its body filling the floor of the stern. Its huge tail flopped over the side, dangling in the water. I tried to remove the fish-hook but then realized that it had swallowed it and gave up. I cut off the branch-line.

'It's a good job he got caught; he wouldn't have left us a single fish and would have ruined the long-line. He's delayed us, though; we should have finished by now,' said my old man.

He took the main-line out of my hand and got back into the *fournos*. He bent down and rinsed his bloodstained hands in water and then began to haul in the line again. I took up the oars once more and rowed backwards constantly; our bow continued to face westwards. He brought in a few hooks. He felt the line coming in without any resistance.

'The fucking bastard has snapped it ... There again it might have been the current, which was dragging you off course ... Anyway, only a few hooks – four or five – have been left down there,' he said, looking at the coils of main-line spilling out of the basket.

'Let's go to the first lamp,' I said and I picked up the crank to get the engine going.

'Hang on ... just a moment ... look over here on the left ... next to you ... there's the central buoy-line with the stool half-sunk in the water. Fortunately we can carry on hauling in the line by moving before the wind, along with the current.'

By the time I had rowed the boat up to it, the severed main-line had come up to the surface. He examined it carefully in the lamplight.

'The dogfish was pulling hard, fighting for his life, so what do you expect? The main-line rubbed against the bottom, on the coral, and snapped ... Row hard backwards ... '

I brought the boat up to the half-sunken stool, he bent over, picked it up, rapidly hauled in the buoy-line and placed it with its sinker in the stool. I took the stool from him and placed an empty basket in front of him. He put the piece of main-line from the first long-line in it, quickly tidied up the ends of the two long-lines and then carried on hauling in the line.

'Move her away ... row hard backwards, there's something tugging on the line ... well done, that's it!'

He brought a few more hooks in and then a stone bass came up out of the water. He tried to remove the hook that it had swallowed.

Suddenly he stopped. Still holding the fish, he put his two hands together over the lamp to cut out the glare and gazed out to sea.

Suddenly, he shot up like a spring, let go of the fish and quickly shoved the basket in front of him out of the way; it all fell into the sea and was lost. Springing out of the *fournos* like a madman, he shouted at the top of his voice: 'Turn the bow round to the north, quickly, row back with one oar and forwards with the other! Turn the bow round to the north ... turn the bow round to the north ... get your bow round to the north!'

I rowed as hard as I could. From the open sea came a dull roar, which was growing louder and louder. I had scarcely managed to turn the boat round when the first wave crashed into us, almost side-on. The boat half filled with water.

# 9

# Portents

A LITTLE EARLIER, round about midnight, Kakkápetris had stumbled out of Klitos' wineshop in the small square by the grocer's store and gone to open up his café, a poky place on the other side of the square. He had paused outside the door for a moment, trying to think. He'd forgotten something... Ah yes, now he remembered... He crossed the road, went into the bakery and picked up a freshly baked loaf of bread, just as he did every night.

He had lived the whole of his life in this small ancient square. During the daytime he brewed coffee for the grocers and their customers, for the shops roundabout and the bakery.

When darkness fell he would set out on the longest journey of the day: he would cross the square and make his way to his friend's wineshop, opposite the Venetian tower. Usually the bar was full of Englishmen, permanent residents of the little town. At the back there was a wooden frame with about ten barrels on it. He would turn on a tap, fill his glass with wine, sit at one side behind a barrel and gradually sip its contents. If he got into the mood, he would perform his dead man's act, sometimes crying and sometimes laughing. He did a brilliant job: his scrawny body helped him play the part, but even more so his baldness and his long narrow face with its sunken cheeks. After midnight he would get up and go and open up his café. Quite when he slept nobody knew.

Every night, at about this time, he had to serve the harbourmen. It was not so much a job as a vocation, one that he had been carrying out for years. Before they went out fishing they would have a coffee, and he was always there waiting for them, ready to brew it up. He didn't charge them for it: it was enough for him to hear their stories and conversations, and to receive a fish once in a while. In the summertime they would sit outside on the cobbles of the small square. In the winter, however, they would all snuggle into his café, maybe a dozen of them at a squeeze. At such times he would enjoy their company more. He would stand alone behind the counter with his coffee-making implements and run the show like a good skipper. But if there was a storm and they didn't turn up, his spirits would sag. Some said that that was when he slept. They hadn't shown up for over two weeks but tonight they would come for sure, for the sea had been calm since yesterday.

He pushed open the door and went inside, stood behind the counter, picked up the pressure stove and began the process of lighting it. First of all, he daubed some meths above and below the head of the burner and then lit it to heat it up. When the metal was red hot, he closed the pressure valve, gave a few strokes on the pump and then lit it. He watched it for a few moments and then, when he was satisfied, he put it back in place under the *outzáki*,[69] so as to keep the water and sand constantly on the boil so that he could make good coffee and do it quickly. Then he went outside and filled the *kouza*[70] with fresh water from the fountain next to the café.

First came Kefalas and Loullís: he'd seen them drinking in Klitos' taverna and the moment they suddenly decided to become businessmen; they'd been talking it over together, thinking out loud and causing a rumpus. They were assistant fishermen, though they worked as casual labourers and not on a regular basis ... They were going to jack it in, there was no future ... they were going to start up their own business and become gravediggers. They'd fallen out, though, because one of them had to be in charge and take the title of 'director' and there were two of them. Neither of them had given way ... they'd come to blows and the tavern-keeper had driven them out.

'Fix us some coffee ... extra sweet,' ordered Kefalas.

'Out with you, you rogues! Gravediggers – whatever next!' cried Kakkápetris.

He didn't like the prospect of their new business. He was the finest cadaver in town; he'd been practicing for years; everybody acknowledged the fact. That was fine but not Loullís and Kefalas.

'Out with you, mate ... !'

'Don't shout, we've agreed: Kefalas is going to be the director,' Loullís informed him. Make us some coffee and bring it out ... to our funeral parlour.'

One by one, they began to arrive. Kakkápetris got down to work; he didn't ask them what they wanted for he knew how each of them liked their coffee. They began to talk about the fine weather of the last two days, the currents, the previous day's double catches, in the evening and morning, and the new moon that would be born on Christmas Day, together with the Christ child. They were hoping it would be upright, so that it would bring fair weather. If the new moon was upright, the captain could lie down. If the new moon was lying on its back, the captain would be upright; that is to say, the whole month would be a stormy one and the captain would have to stand up to hold the helm.[71] The present moon, now waning, had first appeared lying on its back and so had brought all these storms.

The main topic of conversation, however, was the catch that Christakis had made: the red bream, the blackfish and the white groupers that he'd caught – just amazing! 'Good for him for having had the pluck to do it!' somebody said, and then added, 'God does exist, you know, he was due to give us some fine weather; we haven't had any work for the last two weeks. So be it: the present calm weather came just at the right moment; otherwise, how could we have celebrated Christmas in two days' time?'

The last to arrive was Pateras, although he never drank coffee: it damaged your nerves, like cigarettes, he would say.

'Where's the octopus you promised me?' Kakkápetris asked him.

'I didn't even get one for the mayor. I was out of luck. I went to catch two at midday but they'd all burrowed themselves in and covered their dens with stones and shells ... Bad weather's on the way.'

'Rubbish,' replied Kakkápetris.

'You can sneer if you like but I'll have you know that before it got dark I even saw some seagulls; some gulls came into the harbour, sat on the Koulas and now ... it's very dry; there's no humidity at all ... the floor of my warehouse down in the harbour is dry ... there's bad weather on the way, I tell you, there's bad weather on the way.'

'Pateras is right. When we set our nets at dusk there was no current, but when we went to haul them in at about nine o'clock, the current was like a river; it was moving up in the opposite direction, towards the north-west. It was the current you get before a *tramountána*,' Loukís informed them.

'Are you sure about that? It's moving up, you say?' asked Savvas.

'Yes,' replied Bekiris, 'I set my nets yesterday evening as well, a bit further down from Loukís. After it got dark the current was like a river; it was moving upwards.'

'I'm going to call Charalámbis,' said Savvas, leaving his coffee and suddenly going out to fetch his brother. A few moments later he could be heard yelling at him to wake up.

Nobody showed any sign of leaving. They all waited for him to come and discuss the matter with them because at the end of the day it was he who would decide; he was the one who would say what they should do. They always respected his opinions. He understood; he was good at reading the signs of the weather and interpreting them.

It didn't take long for him to come. As soon as he entered, his coffee – he liked it extremely sweet – was on the counter. As he drank he listened thoughtfully to the news about the gulls coming in at sundown and sitting on the Koulas in the harbour, about how there was no humidity and how the current had suddenly turned and was moving north-westwards. He questioned those who had set their nets the previous evening thoroughly on this last point.

'A *tramountána*'s coming in, probably about dawn ... there'll be no fishing tonight ... let's go down and get the boats out of the water,' he said.

'But not a single cloud has appeared above Mt Kornos over towards Vasília, nor over the mountains of Asia Minor,' Karmiotis ventured.

'You stupid sod, those are daytime signs, how do you expect to see them at night, especially when there's no moon? You can be sure that in the morning you'll be able to see the mountains of Asia Minor very clearly, if you're not drunk. Then again the *tramountána* might ... I'll tell you, she's a crafty devil, a real swine, a bitch ... She moves with the other weather systems around her; she'll stick to another one nearby ... a nor'-wester or a nor'-easter and then she'll do her damned best to hide her ugly secrets. She gives no warning of her approach; it happens like that sometimes. Hey, Kefalas, go and get Mavromitis to fetch his truck, that old army one with the auxiliary gearbox, so that we can haul the boats out.'

'I'm not going, I'm not a fisherman anymore, I'm a businessman,' replied Kefalas, 'let a fisherman go.'

'Sod you, you bloody fool! Someone else must go,' exclaimed Charalámbis, and he pushed Bekiris forward.

They all set out for the harbour together, their footsteps ringing out on the cobbles like the sound of an army passing. They woke everybody up and nobody dared complain: otherwise how would anybody be able to show their face in the harbour once it was light? They would be scoffed at, booed and get into a lot of trouble. Nobody dared fall foul of the harbourmen and their mocking tongues.

They emerged from Trypití and the harbour appeared in front of them.

'After all the storms we've had, are we going to lose this fine weather?' asked Payiondís, but he carried on down to the road anyway like everybody else; they were all dispirited and their heads hung. The fine weather and the hope it had brought had not lasted long.

They silently got into their boats, untied the thin ropes that held them fast to the quay and took up the oars. They rowed them over to the stretch of sand below the castle. The harbour was deserted and looked like a graveyard. There were no other vessels, only the fishing boats. They put them in a row, dragging the bows just out of the water, as far as one man could drag on his own. They each placed one wooden slipper under the bow, prepared the rest and waited. They were all there, in a row, except for the *Argo*.

Far off, in the stillness of the night, could be heard the sound of the truck approaching. The tow-rope was prepared – a long thick rope that was long enough to go round both sides of a boat, to pass round the stern and extend beyond the bow so that the whole boat could be pulled without splitting from the strain. First it was placed around the *Astero*. When the truck arrived the thick tow-line was carried high up onto the road and hung onto the back of it. Four people on either side held the boat up straight while the truck towed it forwards about two metres and then stopped so that another slipper could be fed underneath it. Charalámbis directed operations until the bow was drawn up just beneath the road.

'Whoa, easy does it! You'll smash the rocks at that rate! ... Lay her gently on her side! ... Let her belly rest on the sand ... that's it! Let's get them all out and then we'll see what's what,' cried the gaffer.

They worked mechanically, silently and cheerlessly, without the usual banter. The tow-rope was fitted around another boat and the truck moved a little further to the right, opposite its bow, so that it could tow properly, in a straight line. The riff-raff didn't show up: there was silence and gloomy faces; the only thing that could be heard was Charalámbis' voice, tolling like a mournful bell: 'Pull! ... Stop! ... Pull! ... Stop! ... Pull! ... Stop!

The last boat, Bekiris's, was half-way up the beach when things suddenly took a turn for the worse. The first wave could be heard breaking against the lighthouse mole, followed by another and then another. The sea began to ruffle in the harbour. Everybody rushed to stand the boats up straight, to prop them up, to place big round pieces of palm trees under their bellies, barrels, pieces of wood, stones, props and anything else they had gathered together especially for the occasion. Finally, they tied them all up firmly on the beach so that none of them would get dragged back into the sea by the waves.

In that corner the Koulas, on its rocky ledge, provided extra protection. The waves, however, rode over the moles, while others, surging in through the harbour mouth, struck the quay opposite. The foam was thrown high up above the road, struck the walls and the warehouses and then fell back into the harbour, creating more waves and a terrible swirl. They all stayed to help out wherever help was needed; to wedge the supports in more tightly, to tighten the ropes ... despite the rain that began to lash down and the howling wind. They were doing their utmost to protect their livelihood.

Just before daybreak someone brought Charalámbis a message: his uncle, Kapetán Panayís, wanted to see him. He called his brother Savvas over.

'Half of the men can go home to change and take off their wet clothes, but they must come back so that the others can go as well. Some men must stay here all the time to keep an eye on things.'

'Don't worry, but don't be long. Off you go,' replied Savvas, a man of few words. He too realized what was up, for he knew their uncle well.

He set off in the blinding rain to make his way up into the town. He was forced to pass beneath the castle arches and into the moat because the roads around the harbour quays were impassable – the waves were riding over them. He climbed the hill above the police station and made for his uncle's house. The roar of the waves faded a little in the narrow streets above the harbour. When he reached the house, he pushed open the gate and entered the yard. He was standing in the kitchen waiting for him, with the door open.

'A *maïstrotramountána*,' said the old man.

'Yes, a *maïstrotramountána*[72] ... there was almost no sign of it; it struck without warning, the bastard.'

'What about Christakis ... and his son?'

'They're down by Pig Island. It came in at about two o'clock ... they must have been hauling in their lines at the time,' replied Charalámbis.

'Did he have a shallow-water line with him ... to set near the shore?' the old man asked again.

'No, he took only deep-water ones.'

'That's a relief ... then he's set his lines out to sea, by Pig Island, on the same bank where he caught the fish yesterday, that's for sure. He's a sensible bloke; he must have kept out in the open sea.'

'That's what I think,' he said, taking the hot cup of tea from his Aunt Maritsoú. He drank it all in one go.

'Things are not quite so bad after all,' the old sailor continued to himself. Cape Stázousa is only three miles away from Pig Island ... on the whole of the north coast there's nowhere else you can take cover; the only safe place is in Limiónas ... but if you're caught outside ... if you don't make it in time, how can you get in?'

'I'm going home to change. I'll call on Mavromitis again to take me down to Limiónas.'

'Come and pick me up as well, we'll go together.'

'You don't expect me to drag an old man like you around in this weather, do you? There's not only bad weather out at sea, can't you see the rain out here? ... I mean, it's lashing down.'

'What's got into you, Charalámbis? In two hours at the most it'll sweep everything spotlessly clean. A *maïstrotramountána* will unleash a lot of rain in the first few hours but then it clears up, and all that's left is the wind and a heavy sea.'

'You will come and pick him up, won't you, my son? Otherwise he'll get no peace, he won't be able to sit still; he's been up since this wretched storm came in, since two o'clock ... I know it for a fact ... The young lad is also with him. You will come, won't you?' pleaded Maritsoú, who up until then had just been listening quietly.

'Okay, aunty ... I'll drop by. Now I'm off to change,' said Charalámbis, making as if to leave.

Suddenly the gate opened. The small woman who came in was soaked to the skin; her hair and clothes were dripping wet and tears were flowing from her large black eyes. She didn't even greet them.

'I don't know where to go ... or what to do,' she spluttered, looking now at the old man and now at Charalámbis.

'I don't believe it,' broke in the old captain, 'how can a woman like you, someone who's always giving other people courage, who's always saying that God is great and loving, get into such a dreadful state? ... Have you lost your faith in God?'

'But my husband ... and my son?'

'It looks as if you've also lost the faith you had in your husband ... he's a good sailor ... he's no fool ... he knows how to sail the sea and how to ride the waves, however big they are ... I'm sure he's headed out to the open sea, as he should do in a case like this.'

'We're going to Limiónas to fetch them. By sundown they'll be back home,' Charalámbis promised her.

'There's nothing you can do. Go in and get changed and in a while, when the rain has stopped, you can go back home to your children and your work,' added the old man.

He took her by the shoulders and steered her towards Maritsoú, his wife. She followed the old woman with her head bowed, wiping away her tears with the back of her hand. Charalámbis went out into the yard, opened the gate and hastily made his way home: he too lived in the narrow lanes of the Old Town.

The rain began to ease off: the old sailor had been right.

# 10

# Maïstrotramountána

'Hold on tight, don't stop, ride the storm! Aim the bow just left of north and keep it there; for God's sake, don't let it turn you sideways!'

The second wave was bigger, but I just managed to turn the boat round nicely and she rode the wave. The bow suddenly rose up, water came over the top and slammed down onto my face, followed by even more when the boat's belly crashed back down after the wave had passed beneath it. The small vessel rocked quite a bit: as the water ran over her, she swayed from side to side, but she stayed upright with her keel down, and the dead fish swam at my feet.

'Keep the bow facing into the waves! ... Keep the bow facing into the waves! ... Keep your wits about you, mind they don't turn us sideways! ... Look, there's the North Star: don't lose sight of it ... row forwards ... row ... move a bit to the left of it, watch it, try and steer by it ... but more than anything else keep your eye on the waves.'

Along with the heavy sea, a strong wind blew up. I tried as hard as I could to keep the bow facing into the waves, but with the boat half full of water, she was hard, very hard to control; the vessel had become unstable and was weighed down, and the sea was a heaving mass. Another wave came, and then another; the boat began to toss up and down endlessly. My father carefully made his way to the stern, grabbed the iron bucket and began to bail out the water in a series of rapid movements.

'That's it, keep her facing into the waves, hold on tight, hang on, we'll make it ... I'll get the water out. In a moment I'll get the pump.' Suddenly he let go of the bucket. 'As for you, mate, you can fuck off!' he cried and, lifting the shark up by the head, he pushed it into the sea.

Then he raised the triangular floor of the stern, picked up the hand-pump, wedged it in against the engine axle, and with powerful strokes continued to remove the water, which soon disappeared beneath the floor. The boat became a lot lighter – I could feel it, and I could control her a lot more easily. My old man didn't stop for a moment; he kept on pumping out the water, which was now coming in over the bow and the sides.

The wind was howling and the sea was seething, but louder still was the roaring of the waves, which were crashing against the rocks along the coast. Keeping my eyes fixed on the bow, with an oar in each hand, I rowed as hard as I could, sometimes both oars together and sometimes one in front and the other behind, depending on the conditions, so that I could keep the bow turned towards each wave that came looming out of the darkness. The forked stick with the lamp had vanished from the bow; quite when the sea had snatched them away I had no idea.

'Take her out ... take her further out to sea ... keep the bow facing into the waves ... just turn her sideways a bit so that the bow doesn't slice straight into the waves. Watch each wave carefully; try and work out where it's coming from so that you can ride it properly ... That's it, well done! Hold tight and take her out, we mustn't go inshore, move her out whenever you can, away from the land, keep moving her out to sea ... if we're driven into the breakers by the shore nothing will save us.'

He kept calling out in a loud voice so that I could hear him, while constantly working the arm of the pump to get the water out. I didn't let up on the oars for an instant. I merely tried after a while to adjust to the pitching of the sea and get into some kind of rhythm, rowing as steadily as possible but a bit more slowly, for I thought that I would probably have to keep it up for hours on end. Nothing was visible in the thick darkness; neither the land, nor the horizon, only a black mass approaching, looming ever higher. I felt it most keenly just before it lifted us up: I would see the wave just at the last moment before it crashed straight onto the bow, and I constantly struggled to prevent the bow from swinging round, so that the wave wouldn't hit us side-on.

'You're doing a good job ... keep calm ... and keep at it ... we're definitely moving further out to sea ... look, the waves are not so rough ... keep moving her out. The further we get away from the shore the better.'

'Why don't you try and get the engine started?' I cried.

'It's completely flooded; it's a petrol engine, it won't start.'

Even so he picked up the crank and began to turn it. He was right: the engine wouldn't start. He put the crank down, pumped out some water, and then picked it up again, but it was hopeless; there was no response. I couldn't see him as he was standing behind me; I could only hear him, and I didn't dare turn round as I was watching the constant flow of the waves so that as each wave came up I could make the necessary manoeuvres and ride it properly.

'The engine has to be opened up, the water mopped up so that it can dry out, and the spark plug changed. If it was a diesel engine, it would start. It's impossible to do a job like that in these conditions.'

I wiped the water out of my eyes; I couldn't see, and I'd lost the North Star ... I noticed that all the stars and even the sky had disappeared. I thought I saw a flash of lightning, just to the left of the bow, out to the north-west. He must have noticed it as well.

'*Maïstrotramountána ... maïstrotramountána*,' he murmured to himself.

I heard him and I understood. It was the worst type of weather ... on my face, in my body I could feel the heavy seas that run into each other from two different directions and, in a churning mass, sweep down with the strong wind, between the north and the north-west. Soon there would be heavy squalls with thunder and lightning. I'd heard Kapetán Panayís talk about this kind of weather. He would utter the word with a sense of awe. It was vile, the dirtiest kind of weather that a sailor could experience: there was no worse kind of weather than a *maïstrotramountána*!

If only the boat were at least decked over ... Being open like this, every time the bow hit a wave, all the water flew in and struck me on the face.

'Now that we've come a long way out, we can change over,' he said, 'you can take a rest, but be careful, don't let the waves turn us sideways.'

'Stay where you are, I can manage. If I get tired I'll let you know.'

'You're doing fine ... you're in good shape; it just goes to show how useful the gym and the training sessions have been.'

I remembered the daily lecture: 'Give it up ... all this training isn't going to earn you a living!' It had been the same old story every day, ever since the day I'd started training at the track, nearly a year before ... but personally I always longed for the moment my teacher would ask me to do it.

The jolt caused by the sudden pitching of the bow, along with the freezing water, brought me back to reality. This wave was unusually high: it must have been the ninth wave, as the old seafarers say. The biggest wave always comes after a series of eight; if you manage to ride the ninth, the biggest of them all, then you have nothing to worry about. I heard them talking about it and so one day I asked Kapetán Panayís if it was true, but he didn't give me an answer.

The wind was howling in my ears; at times it suddenly grew fiercer and came in gusts with a long drawn-out whine. My ears and nose were frozen yet strangely enough I could feel sweat trickling down my spine. Heavy rain must have set in for at times the water on my lips no longer tasted salty. I was definitely tired now. I suddenly felt anxious because I hadn't heard him call out for a while, so I stole a quick backward glance. He was standing about a metre behind me, holding the tube of the pump in his left hand, as he constantly pressed up and down with his right.

'Can we change over? I think I've had enough.'

'Hold on a bit longer, I'm coming.'

He put the pump down and, constantly gripping the gunwale with one hand, came and stood by me. He waited a few moments for the bow to rise and then, once the wave had passed beneath the boat, he grabbed the oars with his strong hands.

I went round behind him and began to work the pump, to bail out the water myself. It was hard to get the hang of it; my hands were numb and now there was no need for haste or force – only when a lot of water came in. A short while passed and I began to feel the cold for the first time. I was soaked to the skin; my clothes clung heavily to my body and I felt there was no way they could absorb any more water. If it had been summer, I would have taken them off to relieve myself of the weight. A thick sheet of rain borne on a long gust of wind served to remind me that I still needed them, even though they were soaked through.

Now I was able to take a brief look around me, but in the flashes of lightning only the boat was visible, as far as the bow; nothing else was visible, as if we were in a cloud. I could feel the water falling on me and with my lips tried to make out whether it was seawater or rain. The sea and the low clouds had merged into each other and looked as if they were fused together in a single mass. Jagged streaks of lightning and thunderclaps followed each other in constant succession. The lightning first appeared above, not very high up, and looked like huge stalks with bare branches that lit up and shot over half of the sky. At the same time successive claps of thunder echoed all around. The howling of the wind and the sea could only be heard in between.

The crashing and foaming of the sea gradually seemed to abate; the waves were now definitely more even and we were not being tossed around so much. The roar of the waves breaking against the rocks was growing fainter and fainter; we had come a good way out into the open sea. He was right: it was better like this; the further you got away from the shore, the better.

'Have you noticed how the waves are more even now? Didn't I tell you so?' he cried. 'At times like this only clumsy oafs and fools head towards land ... and a certain drowning. The first thing these waves do on approaching shallow water near the shore is show their awesome power. They swell and rise up and then, when they run up against the seabed, they hit it with all their might, lift up, turn over and scatter everything in their path. Only reefs and rocks can withstand them ... if they are rooted firmly in place. Then they break, turn into foam and hurl themselves onto the land. Whatever they've swept up will be tossed around endlessly and then dashed against the seabed over and over again. Then they dissolve into foam until they finally die out on the shore. But if the water's deep, it's a different story. Then the waves come with all the raw energy of the open sea, strike the rocks and are hurled upwards ... That's when the rocks howl with pain, and not the waves like many folks think. God knows how many times I've heard it; anyhow, that's more or less how it is.'

My father fell silent. In the lightning he looked gigantic and, because of the way he was standing, his body blocked out the wind and the water, protecting me. It wasn't just his frame and his shoulders. That thick woollen overcoat also made him look enormous.

'If you're tired, we can swap over,' I cried, 'I feel cold and a spell on the oars will warm me up. Take that wretched overcoat off, it must weigh over twenty okas. Now that the going's a bit easier, we should change over more often; it'll help the blood to circulate better ... and we'll also save energy.'

I put down the pump, crossed over the top of the engine and went to stand beside him. I waited for two big waves to pass under us and then quickly snatched the oars out of his hands.

'We'll wait for daybreak ... then we'll see what we can do,' he said, moving astern. Before taking up the pump he took off his overcoat and flung it into the sea. It began to rain a lot harder, one squall following another.

'It can't be long before dawn,' I thought. 'It must have been two o'clock when the storm began and more than three hours must have passed since then. I wonder where east is, where the sun will appear ... or rather the light ... perhaps over there on the right ... in the troughs of the waves, seeing as they're coming from both the north and north-west.' I looked towards the east, but there was nothing, not even the slightest sign of day; the waves, the thick rain and the clouds all obstructed the view.

My thoughts turned to the shark. If it hadn't delayed us, we'd have finished hauling in the lines and we'd have been on our way to the harbour when the trouble started. The engine would have been running and things would have definitely been better. Okay, we might have had nowhere to go, no haven to shelter in; we'd have headed out to sea. We certainly wouldn't have entered the harbour ... The harbour mouth is broad and faces the full force of northerly gales. The waves would be riding up onto the lighthouse and the moles.

The fishing boats will have been smashed to pieces, at least all those that were afloat ... this nor'-nor'-wester not only came in very suddenly but it also came in without any warning; everybody was fooled, for sure. Unless there had been warning signs in the harbour itself ... I remembered how the seagulls had behaved the previous evening before sunset ... the dryness at midnight, the strong current flowing in the opposite direction ... Yet the one unmistakable sign, the surest warning of a *maïstrotramountána* had not appeared: the mountains of Asia Minor had not been visible on the previous afternoon. I had noticed my father looking out in that direction time and time again. The shark was definitely to blame, it had delayed us ... now that had gone too ... and that superb tail ... how I would have liked to have had its huge tail; I would have dried it in the sun and then hung it up at home.

The darkness began to lift, revealing the thick shafts of the rain, and I was now able to see beyond the bow. There were still flashes of lightning and claps of thunder but they were no longer occurring together; there were intervals in between them which were growing longer and longer. A short while ago, after each flash of lightning the thunder had sounded just before I managed to count to five; now it was sounding after I'd counted to ten ... they were definitely moving further away. It was getting lighter all the time: the sun would come out again today and would do so despite all the efforts of the sea and the rain to stop it ... except that it wouldn't be strong enough to warm us.

'We've lost the rudder!' my old man suddenly exclaimed from the back of the boat, 'we lost it during the night without realizing it, even though, as well as being secured by its pintles, it was also fastened to the boat with wire.'

'After the storm set in, the boat was tossed up and down a lot and took a good beating,' I cried, without turning round to take a look.

'Ah well, we've got no engine anyway, so it wouldn't have been any good ... With the daylight the storm has died down a bit, although I don't think it'll stop completely,' I heard him say in an effort to persuade himself otherwise.

It was true, the wind was no longer howling and the waves, which were now clearly visible, though big – four or five metres high – were more regular, almost even. Rowing took less effort though a lot of care, once a wave had passed beyond the stern in order to continue, with unabated force, its journey in towards the land.

Together with the wind, the rain had also eased off, after falling continuously since the moment it had started. I stole a backward glance towards the land but couldn't see anything, perhaps because of the rain, or the distance ... We must have come a long way out.

The light grew stronger: day had well and truly broken. Through the thick shafts of rain dense black clouds were visible drooping down low onto the rough and stormy seas.

11

# Near the Cape

I WAS STANDING AT THE STERN, occasionally bailing out water when I noticed a thin strip of light to the north that was gradually getting wider and higher. Rays of sunlight appeared to be shining through it.

'It'll clear everything; it'll drive all the clouds away and leave the sky spotless!' he cried, as he continued to control the boat with the oars.

About an hour passed: the bank of black clouds was rising higher and higher above the horizon, and the rain had stopped. First the mountains of Asia Minor appeared, looking incredibly clear and close, with a band of deep blue above them – a crystal-clear sky – which was continually expanding. The clouds were rising... and continued to rise until the sun appeared. They drifted overhead and then began to slide away towards the south, vanishing behind Pentadaktylos, which, freshly washed by the rain, gleamed like a new pin, its foothills a lush green. Then another strip appeared – a broad one all of foam – and the distant sound of waves pounding on the shore could be heard.

'Come and take over the oars so that I can see where we are. Don't go out any further; hold her steady, facing into the wind. Face straight into the *tramountána*: now and again you can turn slightly but make sure you don't let her see the side of the boat.'

I took up the oars but found it hard going, and it took me a while to get back into my rhythm as my hands and feet, indeed the whole of my body was frozen stiff.

'Astern of us, right where the waves are heading inland, must be Cape Stázousa – you can see the break in the mountain high up behind it – though I'm not sure. We're three or four miles out and you can't see the cape from here.'

'Let's go inshore to make certain,' I suggested.

'We'll go in a bit but we must be careful. Keep your bow facing into the wind. That way the bow will cleave through the waves and not run completely against them. Let the waves take you towards the shore and carry you with them, but be careful, do it gradually and don't let the waves turn you sideways.'

I let the boat be carried along by the waves as he had told me. I made sure they didn't turn us sideways when they lifted us up, and took extra special care on the descent, when the waves rolled away beneath the stern. The *Argo*'s bow was not wedge-shaped but slightly rounded: the vessel had been designed more for riding the waves. God bless the boatbuilders of Syros!

'That's it, well done, we're being carried along nice and quickly. Mind out, though, make sure the bow is always facing into the wind: it's daytime and you can see well now.'

'It's much harder,' I replied. 'Especially when the waves pass under the boat.'

The pounding of the waves was growing louder and clearer all the time: we were nearing the shore. It was another way of calculating the distance. The sun rose high in the sky; it was getting near midday. Our frozen bodies warmed up a little, and the wind helped by almost drying out our clothes and loosening them from our skin. I could now pick out the sound of each wave breaking on the rocks – I felt I could count them. Meanwhile my old man lifted up the cover and inspected the engine.

There was nothing doing: as the boat went up and down, any water that got in would be thrown upwards and so the engine was constantly flooded. He replaced the cover and then, taking hold of the pump, secured the bottom of it with a thin rope, just as he had tied the top of it to the seat, so that it would stand up on its own without having to be held. When he had finished he stood up again.

'Yes, that's Cape Stázousa all right,' he said to himself. 'You can see the high rocks with the waves breaking against them; the water is deep right up to the shore and so the waves travel at full force, throwing up clouds of spray when they hit the rocks.'

He fell silent. I knew without looking that he was standing behind me and studiously surveying the cape that was drawing ever closer. He knew all too well that we wouldn't be able to last much longer, after being soaked to the skin for hours, our bodies worn out by fatigue and lack of sleep, and numbed by the wind and the cold. We – both ourselves and our beautiful boat – had far surpassed the limits of our strength and endurance. We had held on determinedly, we had fought bravely, we had unerringly ridden all the waves – and they were not few in number, they were endless. The open sea had also been good to us, it had saved us, but it wouldn't be long before another freezing night set in.

He had to make a bold decision: the high headland was clearly visible, as were the waves that were constantly beating against it. To the left, the sections of wave that didn't strike the headland appeared to continue, to travel a little further on, and then break and foam before dying out on the low shore opposite, about half a mile beyond the cape. Behind the high rocks of the headland lay Limiónas, the only refuge from all the foul weather of a northerly gale on the whole of the north coast.

'But where does all that water go – the water carried in by the waves from the open sea? It doesn't go up Pentadaktylos, that's for sure,' I wondered out loud.

'It goes back to its source, but deep down, along the seabed, in exactly the opposite direction to the water carried along by the waves on the surface.'

'That's what your uncle, Kapetán Panayís, says; that's how the sea's local currents begin.'

'Forget about all that for the moment,' he said, 'and listen: go slowly in towards the shore, just as you are, keeping your bow facing into the waves. Keep to the right of the cape, about twenty metres away where the water is deep, just where the waves are carrying on towards the shore without breaking or foaming. I'll keep a look-out and when I call out, I want you to turn her quickly and forcefully to the left, towards the west, and then enter the bay behind the cape. D'you understand?'

He came and stood by me and suddenly snatched the oars out of my hands. I was startled, but I didn't react.

'You have a good rest, and take in what I told you. Take a good look as well at the lie of the land and where the waves are breaking ... I'll let her drift some more ... and when we near the cape I want you to take up the oars. You just keep looking straight ahead, at the waves ... and I'll keep a look-out over here ... I'll tell you what to do!' he cried.

I went to the back of the boat, where I stood and carefully began to do as he had told me. It was true: the foamless waves, flowing at full force, were crashing against the blackened rocks. There was a loud roar and the spray was hurled upwards, higher than the headland. There it was caught and scattered by the wind, some of it falling downwards. The broken waves carried on towards the shore. But how was it possible to round the cape? How was it possible, how much power did you need to get off or away from those waves in order to turn and get into the long narrow bay of Limiónas?

'Sit down, why are you standing up? I said you should take a rest so that you can think clearly.'

I sat down on the seat in the stern. I noticed that the tiller, carved like a rope, was missing, and then remembered that the sea had torn it off along with the rudder. Now the boat was pitching up and down and shaking more violently. We had drawn quite close to the cape. I didn't feel as if I'd rested: my body was still frozen stiff. Half an hour must have passed. He was holding the boat in position on the waves, while at the same time allowing it to be carried along by them as they headed towards the land.

'Come on,' he said, turning round, 'Cross yourself first. You know we have no other choice ... If we set foot on land you can go and light a candle to the Glykiótissa ... I'll go to Chrysokava.'

He had remembered the Holy Mother: he was sending me to the Panayía Glykiótissa, who was a source of refuge and comfort for all men, while he himself had vowed to light a candle to the Panayía Chrysokava, who had always been the seafarers' strength and shield, who for centuries had been buried deep in the wild rocks of the headland to the right of the harbour, in the catacombs of Chrysokava.

I did as he had told me. I crossed myself, went and stood behind him and, at the first opportunity, took over the oars. It was now harder to hold the boat against the waves, which were growing stronger and higher as we drew closer to the cape. Before going astern, he stooped down and threw all the fish lying at my feet into the sea. Then he dug out a rope from under the bow and, bending over the deck, passed one end through the bow ring. Then he made his way to the stern, constantly holding both ends of the rope. He paused for a while to look at the cape. Without turning round, I realized that he too was crossing himself.

He fastened one end of the rope to the ring on the stern-post and the other to the curved handle of the iron bucket, which he tossed into the sea. When the first wave passed the rope appeared out in front as it tightened both outside and inside the boat – it was threaded through the bow ring. The bucket, now full of water, lay about twenty metres away from the bow. With the next wave the rope grew even tighter and the bucket, as it was dragged through the water, began to act as a brake, whilst at the same time keeping the bow firmly fixed onto the oncoming waves. Then my father, as he stood at the stern, began to pull it. He brought in a little rope and then paid it out. Then he did the same thing again. The iron bucket was acting as both a brake and a movable anchor: it worked perfectly. The effect was immediate: a lot less effort was required, and the boat was being carried along more slowly and steadily, with the bow turning nicely into the waves all by itself. Now I was able to control it much more easily.

'Move her away from the cape a bit and move the stern a little bit to the right when the waves pass under us ... pull a bit on your left oar ... now straighten her up, you're okay now.'

As we drew nearer the cape the swell of the waves increased.

But the oars on the one hand and the anchor-brake on the other kept the bow facing steadily into the waves. We had to manoeuvre again, this time to move even closer to the cape. I didn't find it hard. When we needed to align ourselves with the waves, he helped me by pulling on the rope of the anchor-brake. We were getting quite close: the waves crashing against the rocks were not only being hurled upwards but were whipping up a frenzy of foam around the headland. What was left of them surged on towards the shore, rising even higher. The waves were coming in a steady flow, at long intervals, with the deep furrows between them between twenty and thirty metres wide – surely a good thing, I thought.

Two waves lifted and pushed the boat even further back. I thought for a moment that we were even higher than the rocks, and then we suddenly plunged down, into the abyss. I held on tight, working the oars and leaning my waist against the taut rope that ran towards the front of the boat: in this way the *Argo* was held firm, facing straight into the next wave. The bow was lifted right up: the boat seemed to be taking off and was almost vertical, with its stern low down. I was tilted backwards but did not fall: my back was resting against the engine cover ... and I kept my grip on the oars. I looked to my left and saw the rocks of the headland: they looked lower but were now right alongside us. When the boat came down and straightened out again it was facing north-west. The anchor-brake had worked really well.

'Come on, come on, turn her in, pull one oar forwards and the other back ... quickly, turn her in, turn her in!' he cried at the top of his voice.

At the same time he pulled on the rope, bringing it all the way in until the bucket came up onto the bow. Summoning up all my strength, I worked the oars as quickly as I could and the bow turned to the left towards the mouth of the bay.

'Come on, now row forwards with both oars, hold on, row hard, just as you are ... row ... row ... !'

I mustered all the strength I could and even used my own body as a lever, leaning over the oars. I must have made five or six long and powerful strokes ... The boat had definitely turned towards the bay, which was now clearly visible. We were low down between two waves: one was losing height and moving away towards the shore, while the other was coming towards us, growing higher all the time. Slackening the rope with the bucket on it, he cried out:

'Turn her back onto the wave, pull one oar forwards and the other back, as hard as you can ... turn her, come on, come on!'

I turned the bow but not as much as I should have done, and the wave, as it lifted us up, struck us hard on the right-hand side just behind the cheek of the bow and briefly swept us along with it. Water rushed in and the wave began to turn us sideways and lifted us as high as we could possibly go. When it began to drop sharply on moving away, the right-hand side of the boat suddenly swung upwards while the other sank down and water rushed in over the gunwale: the *Argo* was listing and filling up with water. The oars flew out of my hands and I too was knocked over and fell onto the gunwale.

I grabbed the rope which at that very moment tightened in front of me. Fortunately the iron bucket had slipped from the bow into the sea, filled up with water and begun to act as an anchor all by itself.

I hung onto the rope. I was up to my waist in water but kept a firm grip on the rope and then grabbed hold of the gunwale. My old man, who had also been thrown over in the stern, was struggling to get to his feet. Before the wave had passed completely under the boat I had climbed back inside and picked up the oars again. The rope attached to the anchor-brake grew even tighter, the boat shuddered and the bow suddenly swung round onto the waves, towards the rocks of the headland, which I could now see directly in front of me ... Just a few more metres ... just a few more metres ... a few more metres in, I thought to myself. My father saw me get up and when I picked up the oars he quickly pulled in the whole rope until the bucket clanged as it jammed against the bow ring.

'Hold on, get a good grip on the oars ... row hard forwards, turn into the bay ... move well in, come on ... row ... row ... row ...'

With the boat half-full of water, I now turned round to sit with my back to the bow for the first time so that I could get more power by pulling on the oars and not pushing against them. I rowed one oar backwards and then grasped the other, left oar in both hands, angled it deep in the water, placed one foot on the engine cover and pulled on the oar with every last ounce of strength in my body to turn the boat into the bay ... There was a loud crack and I was suddenly and violently thrown onto the floor, dashing my ear against the foredeck. I could feel the warm blood oozing down the back of my neck.

The oar had snapped in two, breaking in the middle where it had strained against the oarlock. Listing over and out of control, the boat began to whirl round in the swirling foam, shuddering and bashing against the waves as water rushed in on all sides, even the water thrown up by the headland. Even so, it remained upright, with its keel facing downwards. The roaring of the waves striking the headland and the sound of those breaking and dying out in the shallows opposite, together with the howling of the wind, had suddenly become audible again after the blow. Strange, because for quite a while before that I'd heard nothing.

As the boat whirled round for about the third time, and I lay stretched out with my head resting on the deck, I vaguely saw a thick rope land on the bow. Without getting up, I stretched out, seized it and, as I lay there, began to wind it round the bow stem with my right hand. In my other hand I held the loop that was formed at the end of it. I felt the rope tauten and then draw tight around the bow stem. Suddenly I felt an excruciating pain. The thick rope was also tightening around the fingers of my right hand; I could feel them being crushed against the bow stem. My eyes clouded over; I couldn't see a thing. I just tried to pull my hand free ... I pulled and I pulled ... again and again ... I could feel the flesh tearing away.

# 12

# At Limiónas

THE OLD CAR MADE AS IF to stop on the road above the half-ruined carob warehouses by the sea, but the driver started the engine up again and turned right, taking the road that led up to the village of Chartzia. He drove about six hundred metres up it and stopped. Below glistened the angry heaving sea: the first breakers were about a mile out and they were rolling in towards the land, their contours reflecting the irregular lines of the shore. Their foamy crests sank lower and lower until they finally died out on the white pebbles of the beach in front of the warehouses. A mile out to sea the rocky outline of Pig Island occasionally peeped up above the waves: it was there that the waves were starting to break and foam. The rain had stopped and the wind had scattered the clouds.

'I told you to stop down by the warehouses and you've come up the mountain,' Charalámbis remarked.

'That was a fine spot to choose, down by the sea; can't you see all the water the wind is bringing in? That's sea water: it'll rot the bodywork,' Mavromitis complained.

'Up here you get a better view,' broke in Kapetán Panayís.

All three of them got out of the car. They gazed at the sea without speaking. They could see nothing but big waves and foam, for the visibility at sea level was pretty bad. The strong wind carrying spray from the sea was tiring and painful on the eyes. They stood there for a long time, looking out to sea.

'You can't see a thing. Let's go to Limiónas instead, behind the cape. That's the only place they can get in. They might have made it; besides, there are fishermen there as well, local folk ... they might have seen something,' suggested the old seafarer.

'Right, Mavromiti, let's go,' agreed Charalámbis.

They got into the car, turned right and followed the narrow winding coast road that continued eastwards. They drove up and down another two ravines, whose lower slopes were strewn with myrtles and oleanders, while the upper ones were dotted with old carob trees and olive trees with brown or black-and-white trunks full of hollows. The hillsides and hilltops were littered with freshly broken branches. Wherever the car went startled blackbirds shot up into the air. They passed the turning which led up to the head village of Aï-Grosi and continued along the narrow strip of asphalt. As soon as the dirt road leading to Limiónas appeared, they turned off, bearing left towards the sea. Despite the prolonged rainfall, the strong wind had almost dried the earth.

They had gone about a mile when the large bay of Melantrina came into view. When they drew closer, Limiónas appeared beneath them, a smaller bay within the large one, shielded to the north and west by the high headland, which rose and stretched eastwards to a distance of almost half a mile from the innermost part of the bay. The land in front of the mountains protected it from all the southerly gales. They descended a short way, following the southern side of the cape, and stopped. Lower down, in front of them, appeared ten or so flat roofs, the hovels of Limiónas, wedged into the southern slopes of the headland, all with a terrace at the front facing the bay, covered by a brushwood canopy.

Fishermen from the three neighbouring villages had come and settled here permanently. Before that they had used to come down from the mountains and ravage the area, desolating the sea with dynamite. In time they came to love the place and decided to stay for good. They became fishermen – even a few who had only one hand, but they got by. Their home villages, lying high up in the foothills of the mountain far away from the shore, were inconveniently situated. They began to stay at the leeward haven of Limiónas. In the course of time they moved their households and entire families down, and everybody would help out with emptying the nets, rigging the boats, mending the nets, and launching and hauling in the boats. Two of them fished together with their wives and didn't need any helpers, even though one of the women had a belly like a whale: if she had to, she'd give birth in the boat. Limiónas filled with children, which God provided in generous abundance. Now they were squabbling with a few villagers from Aï-Grosi, who still wanted to come and blow up the sea with dynamite, to kill and scatter the fish, which were their livelihood.

Right at the bottom near the water's edge lay six boats, drawn up onto small makeshift mounds. The murky and almost calm waters of Limiónas, full of all the dross that the waves had swept up off the land, flowed back and forth in the strong swell. From the cape could be heard the sound of the waves dashing furiously against the high rocks, and then the sudden din of the water as it showered back down onto the rocks, the scanty soil and the flat roofs of the houses.

Dogs began barking. By the time they had stopped the car was surrounded by children of all ages, all of them barefoot, with even a few goats in their midst: there was pandemonium. Far below three men appeared, climbing up the narrow path, which was studded here and there with stone steps. They quickened their pace when they saw Charalámbis and hastened to approach, pushing the children, dogs and goats aside.

'Hello there! Come and have a drink to warm yourselves up,' said Chrysostomos, the oldest fisherman, a short, fat middle-aged man who was virtually bald.

'Have you seen a boat by any chance, or heard anything?' Charalámbis inquired.

'No, but we know your brother's down there. He's been working in these waters for the last two nights, and he's got trapped there. At midnight last night we all set our nets and then came back to Limiónas planning to haul them in after dawn. About two o'clock disaster struck; the whole lot's at the bottom ... we're ruined,' said Chrysostomos.

'If you set your nets out deep, don't worry, you'll only have suffered a bit of damage. But those who set their nets in shallow water might as well forget the lot,' said Charalámbis.

'Like the night before, Christakis set his lines some distance away from Pig Island, and as there was no moon the lamps on his buoys shone out over the calm sea like two big moons,' Chrysostomos replied pensively. Then he noticed Kapetán Panayís sitting in the car deep in thought and said, 'Come on down out of the wind; the captain can sit down as well.'

'Have you seen or noticed any bits of wood round here, any pieces of boat? Charalámbis persisted, ignoring the invitation.

'No, nothing, we've seen nothing at all. We've been combing the beaches since morning and we've also let the police at Aï-Grosi know. We split up into two parties. The other one, the one that headed eastwards down there, hasn't come back yet. But won't you come down?'

'Okay, take the old man down with you. Mavromiti, you come with me,' he said, opening the door for his uncle to get out.

'Hold on tight, don't get carried away by the wind!' he called out to him.

'The headland is high; it's the best place for a look-out point. The water's deep and there are no breakers offshore,' replied the old man.

He followed Chrysostomos and they went right down to the bottom, close to the water's edge. He glanced at the small boat drawn up onto the beach. He paused for a while on the terrace with its stone seats and brushwood canopy, in front of the house's only room. It was big: the inner wall, facing into the headland, the rear and the flat roof were God's creations, formed out of the solid rock. Chrysostomos had built only the front and half of the side wall. In the first he had placed a door and in the second a window. He had made use of the living rock of the local hillside and left the place unscathed. Inside there was plenty of space for his household goods and the whole family, including his eight children and even his mother-in-law.

Outside on the wall hung the semicircular tin wash-basin full of water, with its small tap stuck just above the base, next to the soap-case with its green bar of soap.

Inside, next to the window, burned the fire, with an old woman seated on a cane stool now poking the logs and now stirring the cooking-pot. On the left a paraffin lamp hung on the wall, next to strings of pomegranates. Underneath, against the wall, stood two large *kouzes* full of water, and above, hanging from the rock ceiling, was the larder full of loaves of bread and *anarí* and *halloumi*[73] cheeses. The crockery and all the kitchen utensils were crammed next to the cupboard, which was built into the wall, next to the beginning of the rock face. Opposite, just visible, was a small storage jar half buried in the earth, full of olive oil. Nearby, in a hollow in the rock, leaned the holy icons of the Panayía and St Nicholas, lit by a clay oil-lamp.

At the back, inside the clean cave, was the bedroom with five or six rough wooden beds; the left-hand corner, barely visible, appeared to be sectioned off with what looked like a curtain. At the front, near the door, was a table with three or four chairs and a large number of cane stools. In the right-hand corner lay the fishing gear, a few pieces of rope, some buoy-lines, two long-lines and, skilfully spread out over a chair, a piece of fishing-net that Chrysostomos had been rigging up, the last piece that was left.

The old seafarer went in. He was welcomed by a middle-aged mannish woman with a swarthy gypsy-like complexion and swollen belly who offered him a chair. He sat down. Her eldest daughter, a beautiful moon-faced girl aged about sixteen with large black eyes like her mother's, offered him a steaming hot glass of fragrant mountain tea.

'God bless you, my child,' he said as he took the glass of tea from her.

From above came the sound of an engine drawing to a halt and the voices of children running. It was the police sergeant, who had been with the party that had headed eastwards. Charalámbis, who up until that moment had been keeping a look-out with Chrysostomos on the highest rock of the cape, hurried down.

'No sign of anything, we've seen nothing at all. We got as far as Chelónes, a fair distance ... the others are on their way,' the sergeant said, anticipating their questions.

'Did you see or notice any bits of wood anywhere? Any pieces of boat or boat's fittings washed up on the land or on the rocks ... anything floating ... in a cove or near a cape anywhere?' inquired Charalámbis anxiously.

'No, nothing. Nowhere,' replied the other.

'Well then, since no signs of a wreck have been found anywhere, I'm sure they must be out at sea; they headed out to sea and are still battling it out,' said Charalámbis.

'You're tired. Let's go down so you can get a bit of rest. Those two over there will go up onto the highest rock of the headland to scan the sea,' said the sergeant, pointing at two fishermen.

'He's not daft, he knows full well that this is the only place he can get in, the only place where he stands any chance, even if it's just a small one; so long as they can hold out – it's been over ten hours since the storm came in,' Charalámbis said to himself.

He agreed to go down but then stopped short, turned his face towards the north-west and then the north. The wind had dropped a little. It was nearing midday. He glanced at the two fishermen climbing up the rock and then pensively made his way down with Chrysostomos.

Suddenly there were shouts from the terraces above. Everybody rushed outside, both young and old, and began running up to the ridge of the headland to look out to sea.

'There's a boat, there's a boat! ... Sometimes you can see it, then it disappears ... there's a boat!'

Charalámbis ran as fast as he could. He scaled the rock where the two fishermen were standing. Before they had time to point it out, he had seen the boat himself: he knew where to look, between the north and the north-west. He saw a wave lifting the boat up ... then it disappeared ... then it appeared again ... then it vanished again ... then it reappeared. It was far out to sea, not close, but he recognized the vessel at once; there was no mistaking it. He stood still for quite a while with his gaze fixed on where the boat was continually heaving in and out of view. He was deaf to the world: he could hear neither the voices around him nor what they were asking him; even the roar of the waves faded away and he didn't even feel the wind on his face.

As time passed he noticed that the boat was coming closer. It was gradually being carried inshore, towards the cape, with its bow facing into the waves. As the waves lifted it up, neither its side nor its bow nor even the stern could be seen; only its egg-shaped interior, with its partitions and seats, and his brother, the youngest of the family, standing in the middle. It was he who had brought him up, along with Savvas, and acted as a father to him.

'Go down and tell the old man that it's them: I can see them, I'm sure of it,' he called out to the sergeant.

'I'm here behind you, ' replied the old man, 'can you see the young fellow? I can't see very well.'

'I can see him, I can see him ... he's standing back at the stern. Both of them are still on their feet ... but what are they up to? What are they doing?'

His voice suddenly dried up and he froze. Now that they had drawn closer to the cape he could see that his brother was controlling the boat only with the oars; they were approaching the shore without an engine. He realized that the engine wasn't working: the storm must have put it out of action; he knew it was a petrol engine. How were they going to round the cape now when they reached it? How were they going to get off those waves before they started to break, how would they be able to turn in ... ? For a moment he remained motionless and speechless as he watched the boat drawing closer and closer to the cape.

'Chrysostomos ... hey, Chrysostomos! Get a boat in the water, quick ... put a long thick rope in it, ready to use ... and another one with an anchor ... a fully decked boat with a diesel engine!'

'We'll use mine, although it can't go into reverse and it can't hold still either. When it starts up it moves forward; the propellor goes round. Before I put it in the boat I used it for pumping water out of pits ... how are we going to hold the boat still and wait at the right moments?'

'Don't worry, that's my business; I know what to do. Quick, get it into the water. Just make sure it starts up straightaway.'

'It never fails,' replied the fisherman.

'Good, go down with the others and wait for me in the boat. Just you get in, I don't want anybody else. I'll watch from up here and come down when I think I have to, all right? Watch out, there's quite a swell: get two to hold the boat if it sways around in the water.'

'Okay,' replied Chrysostomos, and he ran down the slope with the others.

'You stay with me,' Charalámbis said to the sergeant in a commanding voice and then, turning round, he added, 'As for you, old fellow, go on down or you'll freeze; I'll come down too in a bit.'

# 13

# The Foundering

Standing with the sergeant on top of the highest rock on the headland, Charalámbis was able to survey not only the open sea but also the waters closer in around the cape. He could also look down on Limiónas and see the preparations that were underway for launching the boat. He could see the *Argo* drawing closer and closer. At one point he saw them change places: the son took up the oars, while his brother bent down and rummaged about under the bow; he took something out and made his way to the stern.

Charalámbis studied the cape carefully. He observed the motion of the incoming waves, the broad troughs they left behind them and where the breakers began ... He worked out where they would come in ... There was no other choice: the only place was by the backwash of the first line of waves breaking against the headland. He turned round and saw that down below in Limiónas the boat was ready, floating on the water with Chrysostomos at the oars.

'You stay up here and watch them as they approach. I'll be in the boat as well. When they get quite close, before they go past the cape, signal to us, however you can, either with a shout or a wave ... d'you understand?' he said to the sergeant.

'Okay, you can trust me, don't worry,' the seargant replied.

He cast a final glance at the *Argo*, which was getting closer all the time and now seemed to rise almost right up on the waves, with a large section of the keel below the bow standing out of the water. Anyone would think that it was going to pitch over backwards. When he saw the bucket slide away from the bow and then disappear he gave a sad knowing smile: he had taught him how to do that, it was he who had shown him how. He climbed down from the rock and hastily made his way down the hillside.

Every living soul in Limiónas – the women with their infants in their arms, the children, the dogs and even the goats – gathered on the lowest stretch of land, above the water in front of Chrysostomos' door. The men stood a little further down, almost in the water, with the old mariner in their midst, leaning on his stick. Nobody moved; not a word was spoken. Only a baby cradled in a mother's arms made as if to cry but then fell silent too.

He got into the boat and, running his eye over it, realized that it was an old, weathered vessel, with obvious signs of wear and tear on the deck, the gunwale and the planking. First he looked at the anchor and stowed it away under the bow so that it wouldn't get in the way, with its rope properly coiled so that it was ready for action. Then he took hold of the rope he had asked for, passed one end of it through the ring on the stern-post, pulled it through and nimbly tied it low down inside the boat. On the other, free end he tied a bowline knot, gathered the rope up in loops and laid it down carefully on the foredeck. When he had finished, he grasped the oars that lay ready in the rowlocks.

'I'm going to turn her towards the cape, and I want you to start her up and stay at the helm. You open up the throttle and keep taking her round Limiónas in circles and each time you go round get as close as you possibly can to the breakers at the end of the cape, and don't be afraid ... okay?'

'Okay,' Chrysostomos replied with some hesitation: only yesterday he'd lost his nets; he'd set all of them, all ten of them, out in the shallows.

Charalámbis turned the boat's bow to face east. At the first turn of the crank the engine roared into life and the boat began to move, the vibrations of the single-cylindered engine sending shudders through the small vessel. Charalámbis steered the boat with the oars until Chrysostomos went to the back, got into the *fournos* at the stern and took up the tiller. The small boat rocked in the swell of the water in the bay, swaying from side to side.

'Open her up a bit more; the engine will work better and stop shaking ... Now start taking her round Limiónas in circles ... don't be afraid, I'm with you.'

The man obeyed: he did not come from a long line of seafarers. In his youth he had been a shepherd on Pentadaktylos. He had learnt everything he knew virtually by himself without a teacher. He was good at fishing, although he had never seen the sea like this before; even so, he had guts and was smart. He opened up the throttle: the slow shuddering of the engine quickened pace and the boat moved more quickly, its stern dropping deep down into the water. He began to take her round in circles, as he had been instructed: at first small circles within the bay, far from the breakers at the head of the cape, and then five or six larger circles, each time moving further out. His companion let the oars drag in the water, slung in the oarlocks next to him.

'Come on, move her further out, make a bigger circle ... take her up by the breakers ... don't be afraid if we get drenched!' he cried.

He kept one eye on the sergeant standing high up on the rock above them and the other on the breakers down by the headland. The circle grew larger, they went round twice more and were soaked by the water raining down from above, which increased as they neared the head of the cape. Fortunately the boat was decked over; it had only one opening in the middle where there was just enough room for one man to stand up and row, so it let in little water.

'Take her up to the foam made by those waves breaking over there, by the cape ... go on, go on ... that's it ... keep going ... just behind the last high rock at the head of the cape!' Charalámbis was yelling at the top of his voice so that his companion, who was sitting at the helm about two metres behind him, could hear him. All the time his gaze kept swivelling up and down.

'That's good ... now steer whichever course you think is best; make the circles bigger or smaller so that you can get up to the cape, and hold her there right next to that high rock, near where the waves are breaking and the other halves are carrying on towards the shore ... can you see – in the wide gap between the waves? D'you understand? So if we have to, we'll be able to move out a bit and get close to them ... Come on, try it.'

His companion stood in the *fournos* at the stern and made no reply. He steered the boat round in circles as he watched the waves – one half of each wave breaking against the headland, while the other carried on towards the shore. They were all getting higher and they kept advancing in a steady flow. That helped. It didn't take much of an effort: as soon as a wave passed and they entered the broad trough behind it, he would speed up or slow down the engine, steer in a smaller circle if necessary and manage to keep the boat in line with the head of the cape.

Suddenly the sergeant up above began to wave his arms rapidly and shout, 'They're coming in, they're coming in, they're coming in!' His shouts never reached them; they were drowned out by the roar of the waves. The man in command realized that the moment had come ... he must have remembered his Creator for his lips moved, no doubt whispering a plea.

Near the head of the cape appeared the *Argo*, her bow facing into the waves as she was swept forcefully along. Suddenly her stern sank deep into the water and her bow rose higher and higher as if she was going to take off, her keel sticking out in mid-air. By the time the wave had brought her down they had managed to slip into the same trough as her behind the cape. At the same moment they saw the *Argo*'s bow turn towards Limiónas as it began its next turn. It seemed to make some headway, to move a little further in, and then they saw it begin to wheel round again to face the next wave, which was rising higher and higher as it approached. They had almost completed the turn when the new wave appeared to hit the *Argo* on the cheek of her bow, turning her slightly over and then lifting her up, causing one side to sink under and take in water. They saw one of the occupants hanging over the side. Charalámbis breathed a sigh of relief when he saw the figure climb up and get back in as the wave rolled away beneath them, and then take up the oars again. He felt reassured when he saw the *Argo*'s bow turn back onto the waves.

On the next turn, as the following wave began to rise, the two boats drew closer together. Charalámbis noticed the oar snap and saw the *Argo* begin to whirl round.

'Take her round again, take her round, and when the next wave has passed by move her out, get as close as you can to them, and then head back in straightaway! We won't get another chance ... d'you understand? ... Head back in ... we won't get another chance!'

He shouted as hard as he could at Chrysostomos, who was beginning to make the next turn. He cast a quick glance at the oars and in his right hand carefully took hold of the rope, which lay in loops on the deck in front of him, as he had placed it. He watched the *Argo* whirling round in the swirling foam, and the oncoming wave, which was rising higher and higher.

'Take her up close, get nearer ... When the wave has passed under them get closer ... closer.'

The wave struck the *Argo* as it whirled round half-submerged in the water. It caught it on the bow, shaking it violently, and lifted it up, flooding it with foam. As the wave rolled away beneath it, half of the boat was left hanging in the air, and then it plunged down and crashed into the foam at the beginning of the next trough. With its bow now pointing north-west, though half-submerged, it was still floating properly, fortunately with its keel facing downwards in the right position. At the same moment Chrysostomos approached its stern from the left. He eased off the throttle and slowed down when he saw Charalámbis bend down, turn his strong body a little to the left, then stretch out and hurl the rope that was coiled in his hand into the *Argo*. He watched to see if it had landed properly, if anyone had grabbed hold of it, but above all to allow a bit more time, as much as he possibly could.

'Open her right up and head back in ... give it all you've got, they've caught it ... they've caught it ... open the engine right up ... take her in ... take her in ... take her innnn ... !'

He yelled out over and over again; he had seen me grab the rope and he'd seen me coil it around the bow stem. He took up the oars and began to help out. The rope suddenly tautened. Fortunately it didn't only run through the ring on the stern-post but – cleverly and with expert seamanship – was securely tied low down inside the boat. The small boat suddenly jolted, jerked backwards and stopped. The rope slackened. The *Argo* was bigger and full of water.

'Head back in ... head back in ... come on, open the engine right up ... we've done it, they've caught it, they've caught it ... we've done it ... head back ... take her into the bay ... take her innnn ... !'

He let go of the oars and turned his back to the bow so that he could see the half-sunken *Argo*, and then he seized them again and began rowing with all his might to assist the small engine. The rope tautened once more. The two boats began to move towards Limiónas.

Another wave followed but now the boat with the engine was further inside the bay and protected by the high headland; as it swept by, it caught only the *Argo*. She was struck again but this time only on the stern and the wave didn't lift her up; rather it rolled over her and her bow slid round to face the next oncoming wave. In front of her, the boat that was towing her jerked back again and once more the rope slackened, but this time only very briefly. The rope tautened again and the two boats began moving again, advancing slowly but surely towards the rocks at the far end of the bay. Chrysostomos stood proudly in the *fournos*. He held the tiller in one hand and in the other, outstretched one, the rope he was pulling: he too was towing the *Argo* along.

Now small waves, the backwash of the waves that were breaking and dying out in the shallow waters opposite, were beating directly against the sterns of the two small vessels and pushing them forward, helping them to get well inside the bay, deep behind the cape, to the innermost part of Limiónas. Two vessels: one ageing but sturdy with an engine and oars, towing the other along on a tight rope about ten metres behind it; the other, the largest of the two, half-submerged but still afloat in the surf, with battered ribs and beams, broken oars and rudderless. Only its stern and bow stem showed above the water, while inside lay two bodies, one at the bow and the other at the stern, only their heads protruding above the surf.

They entered the leeward haven of Limiónas and the two fallen bodies in the half-sunken boat sat up. The one at the bow had difficulty but made it; in his left hand he was still holding the bowline knot at the end of the rope that was coiled around the bow stem of the *Argo*, and he wouldn't let go.

The wind continued to whistle and howl. The water coming over the cape was even stronger than rain: the *maïstrotramountána* was now venting its full fury on the seaworn rocks of the high headland, lashing them angrily and causing them to groan with pain.

It had swept in suddenly at night with a strong wind and high waves, with awesome power, like an earthquake. With the light of day it had gradually begun to subside, to die down. When the time at which it had first burst in came round again it would blow up once more. Day by day, hour by hour it would slowly lose strength and the waves would drop. It would go on until the next day, or the day after that – lasting for three, four or five days at the most – and then the swell would disappear, extinguished by the *maïstros* that would begin to blow.

# Notes

1. Glykiotissa: a chapel by the sea, to the west of Kyrenia.
2. Maïstros: the mistral (north-west wind); a weather system from the north-west.
3. Snake Island or Koufonisi, an island near Glykiotissa.
4. Kombonisi: a small barren islet to the left of the harbour opposite the Dome Hotel.
5. St Hilarion: Aï-Larkos, a peak above Kyrenia with a medieval castle.
6. Rígena: (derived from the Latin word *regina*) a mythical queen of medieval folklore, whose name is also associated with Buffavento Castle.
7. Yele: a dialectal word, probably derived from the Turkish *yallah*, meaning 'heave' or 'move'.
8. Pateras: literally 'father', a nickname for the fisherman Andreas Toumanis, a great octopus-catcher.
9. Trypití: a famous narrow passage high up in the middle of the port leading up to the Old Town. The Kyrenians believed that if a foreigner went through the narrow path of Trypití, he would stay in Kyrenia permanently.
10. Bottom long-line: a line for sea-fishing, about a mile long, to which is attached a series of short lines, each of which is about 50 cm long and carries a baited hook. The whole system is coiled in a wide shallow basket.
11. i.e. 11 nautical miles. In the 1950s, the time at which the novel is set, Kyrenian fishermen used the standard nautical mile (1,840 m) to measure distances at sea.
12. Pig Island: a rocky islet protruding just above the water that looks like a pig.
13. Tramountána: the north wind; a northerly gale at sea.
14. Thick long-line: a bottom long-line made of thick fishing-yarn with large hooks for deep-water fishing.

15   Panegyri: a religious festival in the Greek Orthodox Church (usually the feast-day of a saint), accompanied by festivities of a more popular nature.
16   Akanthou: a large village in the foothills, 24 miles east of Kyrenia.
17   Koukoumara: a narrow-necked pitcher without handles.
18   Severis: Demosthenes Severis, originally of Nicosia, a carob merchant, landowner and shipowner in Kyrenia.
19   Cane stool: actually made of stalks from giant-fennel plants.
20   Blue-and-white flag: the Greek flag.
21   Koula: an ancient Frankish tower in the middle of the harbour.
22   Aï-Grosi: Ayios Amvrosios (St Ambrosius), a large village in the foothills of Mt Pentadaktylos, 18 miles east of Kyrenia.
23   Ta Tria Adelfia: The Three Brothers.
24   Schooners and goletas: types of sailing-ship.
25   Lateen sail: a triangular sail rigged to a wooden yard. Jib: a small triangular foresail.
26   Touloumotyria: made since antiquity, *touloumotyri* is a moist white cheese similar in texture to feta which is stored by hanging in goatskin or sheepskin bags.
27   Levante: the east wind. Ostria: the south wind.
28   Shroud plate: an iron plate fixed to the side of a boat in order to secure a shroud (a rope or cable stretching from the mast to the side of a boat in order to support the mast). Hawse-hole plate: the metal rim of a hawse-hole (a hole in the bow through which a cable or anchor-rope passes).
29   Tsiakkilerí: the first bay to the west of the harbour, which took its name from the pebbles (*tsiakiles*) which were so plentiful there.
30   Trehantiri: a light, fast sailing boat.
31   Salisvourís: a shipowner and captain from Rhodes whose boat was smashed in the harbour.
32   Monofilament: a transparent, synthetic and very strong type of fishing-line.
33   Six fathoms (*orkés* in Greek), i.e. 36 feet.

34  i.e. base no. for 1951 (22) + date (21) + month (12) + 1 = 56. 56 − 30 = 26.
35  Barbary Coast: (loosely) the coast of North Africa.
36  Poupás: an old skipper.
37  Garbís: the south-west wind.
38  Partesou: a corruption of the French word *pardessus*.
39  Kazinieris: the registrar at the local *gymnasion* (junior high school).
40  Casino: actually a card-players' club in a coffee-house near Trypití. Hadji-Gliyóris Demetriades: a big landowner, millowner, merchant and political personality of late 19th-century Kyrenia.
41  Pombarta: bombard, canon (derived from the Italian word *bombarda*).
42  Transom stern: a stern with a flat termination above the water-line.
43  Boom: a long cylindrical wooden pole to which a sail is rigged.
44  Kataklysmós: the 'Festival of the Flood', held each year on the Monday after Pentecost. It is celebrated all over Cyprus, particularly in Kyrenia and Larnaca, with boat races, water sports, dancing, singing and fairs. Some scholars believe its roots are in an ancient festival for Adonis and Aphrodite, the goddess who emerged from the sea.
45  Sail-sheet: a rope for controlling a sail.
46  Triton: a large marine mollusc with a conical shell used as a trumpet.
47  Archangel's Rock: a reef opposite the church of the Archangel.
48  These were actually made of giant-fennel stalks.
49  Sounding-line: a line attached to a weight for measuring the depth of the water.
50  Chartzia: a village in the foothills of Mt Pentadaktylos, 16 miles east of the town.
51  Pezounokremmoí: a steep section of coastline to the east of Kyrenia full of pigeons (*pezounia*).

52  Main line: a long line to which branch-lines are attached at intervals.
53  Sinker: a weight used to sink a fishing-line, sounding-line, etc.
54  Oka: a Turkish unit of weight equivalent to 1.28 kg.
55  Strop: a ring of rope which holds an oar in an oarlock.
56  The Panayia: the Virgin Mary.
57  Grapnel anchor: an anchor with several flukes or hooks, in this case four.
58  Inspect the ship: the verb used in the Greek original is *pratikáro* = to inspect a newly-arrived ship in order to grant it permission (*pratique*) to use the port.
59  Kiámilos: a fishmonger from Kyrenia and a famous folk violinist.
60  Katsellis: Costas Katsellis, a big Kyrenian hotelier and a pioneer in tourist and hotel development on Cyprus. In his Dome Hotel about 1,000 Greek Cypriot Kyrenians were enclaved during the Turkish invasion and for a period of up to two years afterwards.
61  In the 1950s country buses in Cyprus used to have a metal luggage rack across the back measuring about 1 m long, onto which luggage was tied with ropes.
62  Kemalis and Bekiris: two Turkish Cypriot fishermen from Kyrenia.
63  Chatzifotís: a man from Kyrenia who got angry whenever he was whistled at.
64  Karmióhoma: a clay soil from the village of Karmi, in the foothills of Pentadaktylos near Kyrenia.
65  Lambratziá: a large bonfire lit on Holy Saturday, on top of which was placed an effigy of Judas.
66  A buoy or reed was set up on the surface to mark the position of the fish-traps beneath it.
67  Naftikó Kentro: a combined coffee-house and taverna on the waterfront.
68  Pourkoúri piláfi: (also *pourgoúri piláfi*) bulgar wheat pilaf. Prepared from hulled wheat, the grain is steamed until partly cooked then dried before being ground.

69  Outzáki: a device for making Greek coffee. It consists of a shallow copper tray about 60 cm long × 30 cm wide in which fine sand is placed. The back of the tray is joined to a small tank holding up to 3 litres of water. Both the sand and water are heated by a burner placed underneath them. The tank supplies hot water for the coffee, which is then brought to the boil by placing the coffee-pot (*bríki*) on the hot sand.

70  Kouza: a round pitcher with a slightly pressed-in brim and one handle.

71  If the new moon was upright: a popular saying amongst Greek and Greek Cypriot sailors in the Aegean and Mediterranean. See Patrick Leigh Fermor, *Mani: Travels in the Southern Peloponnese*, Ch. 17.

72  Maïstrotramountána: a north-north-westerly wind or gale.

73  Anarí: a type of soft white cheese similar to ricotta. Halloumi: a type of white cheese made with goat's milk and traditionally formed and stored in pitchers.

# Kyrenia Harbour

*Its Boatyards, Shipowners,
Skippers & Maritime Traders
in the 19th and 20th Centuries*

## The Harbour

When the English took over the government of Cyprus in 1878, they drew up plans for the construction of harbours at Kyrenia and Famagusta so that they would be able to assist Turkey in the event of a Russian attack. When this danger passed, in 1890 the English proceeded to construct a harbour at Kyrenia, having previously decided to scale down the work. Basically, they built two breakwaters, one on the east side and one on the west, leaving a 60-metre gap between them as the harbour mouth, which faced north. A little later the quay and two wooden wharves were constructed.

The Customs House was built in 1916. In 1920 the lighthouse at the end of the western mole was constructed. Up until 1920 the lighthouse had been located high up in the north-west tower of the castle.

When the Republic of Cyprus was founded in 1960 the harbour was reconstructed. The north-facing harbour mouth was filled in and a new one was opened up to the east. A new, long eastern mole was constructed (on top of Seirakayiádes, the remains of the ancient harbour), parallel to the north side of the castle, which extends further east.

## Boatyards

During the period of Turkish rule, and perhaps even earlier, the town's boatyards were situated at Mitsí Yialós, below the Church of the Archangel Michael, where the quayside square is situated today.

Later, after the construction of the harbour's western mole and the quay, Mitsí Yialós was covered over to create a breakwater. The boatyards were then moved further west, to Tsiakkilerí Bay. They remained there until 1940, when they fell into disuse.

Much earlier, in Byzantine times, the town's boatyards lay within the present-day harbour (below the police canteen). Remains of them, in the form of arches, still survive today on the wall.

In the early 1900s there used to be a large forge and ironworks in the Tsiakkilerí boatyards, which belonged to Severis, a big businessman and merchant. Here nails, anchors, hawse-hole plates, chains, and shroud plates were made, together with any other pieces of equipment required by boats at that time. The most famous craftsman was Paraschos Michail.

## Boatbuilders

Of the oldest generation of boatbuilders, the best known are the three HadjiDimitri brothers who came from Alayia in Turkey in 1883 with their Armenian mother and Greek father. Also famous were the Fytís brothers. After the Asia Minor Disaster came Mastro Panáos Danezis, Mastro Pantelís, Mastro Matthaios (all three were from Asia Minor) and Mastro Vasilis from Karavostási. The last boatbuilder (an apprentice to Mastro Vasilis) was Mastro Sotiris from Karákoumi. After the Turkish invasion in 1974, Mastro Sotiris was forced to leave and settled in Limassol, where he has been working ever since.

At an earlier period, boatowners would bring in boatbuilders from Symi, Smyrna and several other islands. They would bring their own tools with them, all hand tools: a cross-cut saw, a string-operated drill, a thin narrow handsaw (*vórzoulas*), a thick handsaw (*sikátsa*), a narrow adze and a wide adze, and caulking gear with a wooden mallet. Once the boat was finished, the boatbuilders would leave: that was the policy followed everywhere.

# Skippers and Boatowner-Captains

*Listed in alphabetical order*

*Kapetán Hadjiyiannis Chiotis*
Originally from Chios, he was a skipper and boatowner in Kyrenia in the second half of the 19th century. Grandfather of the teacher Nikos Chiotellis.

*Kapetán Christos Diakou (of Korina) (?–1932?)*
An old seafarer who served on many ships. A friend of cousins Michail Savvas Keleshis and Michalis Michailidis Poupás. From a young age all three were renowned jokers and wags whom nobody could match.

*Kapetán Fytaís*
A Turkish skipper and boatowner who lived in the last quarter of the 19th and early part of the 20th century.

*Kapetán Christophís Hadjichristophís*
A famous skipper and boatowner who lived in the mid-18th century. In 1783 he personally paid for repairs to the Church of the Chrysopolítissa, situated in the Old Town above Trypití.

*Kapetán Nikoliós Hadjichristophís*
Son of Christophís Hadjichristophís. In about 1870 he married Chrystalloú Poérou. As they had no children, they adopted Christophís Kestas. Of the three boats in his possession, the most famous was the *Antigone*, a fast vessel that almost always won the sailingboat races that were held in Kyrenia. As was the custom at the time, the boat itself and the ship's cat shared the same name, *Antigone*.

*Kapetán Hassan Ibrahim*
A Turkish captain from Kyrenia, grandfather of Sapri Tahir, a well known Kyrenian Turkish Cypriot of the 50s and 60s. He owned

the small boat *Kazí*, which was smashed to pieces in the harbour during a northerly gale in 1934. Later he worked on Severis's ships.

*Kapetán Yiannis Vasiliou Karákoulles*
One of the three Vasiliou brothers, who were all wholesale merchants. Skipper of the family's big three-masted ship *Ta Tria Adelfia*, which was wrecked outside Smyrna in about 1885.

*Kapetán Matthaios Kariolou*
Shipowner and merchant, one of the last in Kyrenia. The last ship to sail from Kyrenia, in 1941, belonged to him. Before that it had lain for years on land, in the Tsiakkilerí boatyards.

*Ioannis Kazinieris (?–1910)*
Father of Costas Kazinieris. He was just a child when Hadji-Gliyóris brought him from his village of Paliósophos to help out in his *casino* (a type of coffee-house), which was situated next to Trypití. Later he took to the sea and married the daughter of Kapetán Pagonis. He owned the *Pombarta*, a small sailing vessel. He went bankrupt in 1903.

*Kapetán Savvas Michail Keleshis (1836–1914)*
A giant of a man two metres tall, the eldest son of Turkomíchalos. He worked mainly with the Black Sea ports. One of the worthiest and most famous skippers in the Eastern Mediterranean. He is also said to have been able to predict the weather better than anybody else. He was nicknamed 'the Sea Master' because he loved teaching. He did not allow only his own family the benefit of his knowledge but shared it with the people he worked with. He produced many skippers and seamen.

*Kapetán Michail Savvas Keleshis (1868–1923)*
Eldest son of Savvas Michail Keleshis, a grandson of Turkomíchalos. He worked on numerous ships. The last one was the *Evangelistria*, which was blown up by the French on 6 February 1916, during the First World War, on its way back from Rhodes.

*Kapetán Iraklís Kleanthís*
Son of Kapetán Kleanthís.

*Kapetán Kostís tou Kleanthí (?–1960?)*
Son of Kapetán Kleanthís, one of the last skippers. A renowned master craftsman, skilled in rigging ships and sailmaking. In the last few years of his life, up until 1958, he looked after the yacht belonging to Costas Manglís, which he kept moored alongside the Koulas.

*Kapetán Kleanthís Costa*
He lived in the second half of the 19th century and married Evanthia, Turkomíchalos' daughter.

*Kapetán Christodoulos Konstantinidis*
A skipper and boatowner, son of Konstantís Pagonis and grandfather of the lawyer Christodoulos Konstantinidis and Phryxos Vrachas. One of his boats was the *Ayia Trias*, a launch-type vessel, which was built at Mitsí Yialós before the end of the 19th century. Its first skipper is said to have been Kapetán Panayís Michailidis.

*Kapetán Neoklís Kyriakidis (?–1949?)*
For years skipper on Severis's boat *Digenís*. A grandson of Turkomíchalos and son of Turkomíchalos' daughter Evanthia, he was one of the last of Kyrenia's skippers.

*Antonio Loretti (?–1820?)*
An Italian from Ragusa, he settled in Kyrenia in about 1785. He assumed control of communications between Kyrenia and Constantinople and other Turkish ports.

*Kapetán Alexandros Michail (1840?–1878)*
Son of Turkomíchalos. He drowned off Cape Gata near Limassol when, it was said, he dived off his ship in order to go ashore. That year, 1878, was a turning point, for it was the year the English arrived in Cyprus.

*Kapetán Antonis Michail (1844?–1885)*
Son of Turkomíchalos, he was shipwrecked and drowned off the south coast of Symi in a sudden and terrible southerly gale in January 1885. None of the crew survived, nor indeed was ever found.

*Kapetán Gliyóris Michail (1838?–1875?)*
Son of Turkomíchalos. Married to a woman called Evanthia. Grandfather of Michalis Oikonomos, the last customs inspector in Kyrenia. He was shipwrecked and lost off Sounion in 1875. None of the crew survived, and his body was never found.

*Kapetán Michalis Michailidis, Poupás*
Grandson of Turkomíchalos and son of Kapetán Antonis. His mother was the daughter of Kapetán Konstantís Pagonis. An experienced sailor, for years he was skipper of the *Archángelos*, the large boat belonging to Costas Mitsidis. He had learnt the art of sailing from his uncle, Kapetán Savvas Keleshis.

*Kapetán Panayís Michailidis (1874–1960)*
Grandson of Turkomíchalos and brother of Michail Savvas Keleshis. Senior captain on Severis's ships and last skipper of the passenger and cargo boat *Rigaina*. In about 1920 he built five lighters in partnership with Stavros Konstantinidis. He continued in business up until 1954 in partnership with his nephew, Charalambis Michailidis. The exportation of carobs by lighter was the last big export business to be carried out in the port of Kyrenia.

*Kapetán Konstantís Pagonis*
Son of Euphrosyne, Turkomíchalos' daughter, he was the founder of the seafaring Konstantinidis family in the mid-19th century.

*Konstantís Piklíyiannis (?–1885)*
Owner and skipper of a small ship 40 feet long. He was shipwrecked and drowned in 1885 on his way back from Anamur in Turkey. His corpse, like that of his brother-in-law, was washed up on the shore at Yialousa, where it was buried.

*Kapetán Alexis Michailidis Tsiakourís (1878–1936)*
Grandson of Turkomíchalos and brother of Michail Savvas Keleshis. He quickly abandoned the sea and was better known as a cabinet-maker and carver of church icon-screens.

*Kapetán Turkomíchalos or Kapetán Míchalos Savvas (?–1850?)*
Originally from Cythera, he came and settled in Kyrenia in the early 19th century. A big rough man, he was renowned for his physical strength and his bravery. He was the founder of the seafaring Keleshis family, which produced many of the town's experienced skippers. Of his four skipper sons, three were devoured by the sea. The places where they were shipwrecked and lost (Sounion, Symi and Cape Gata) show how far Kyrenian ships travelled before the end of the 19th century.

*The Vrachas Brothers: Michalis (1899–1962) and Petros (1883–1983)*
They owned the boats *Glykiótissa* and *Chrysokava* around 1930, which were skippered by Michalis Vrachas. They were the sons of Hadjikonstantís Vrachas (1853–1926), who built the tall warehouses and houses on the west side of the harbour (the ones in the centre belonged to Hadji-Gliyóris), and Katina (daughter of Kapetán Turkomíchalos). The founder of the seafaring Vrachas family was Hadjipetros Vrachas (1829–1883) from Zakynthos. He came to Kyrenia in 1849 and married one of the daughters of Papa-Charálambos from Karmi.

*Other skippers, boatowners and traders*
Kapetán Yiannis Samiotis, Kapetán Telemachos Skopelitis, Kapetán Tilkís (Turkish Cypriot).

# Sailors

Hardly any information exists at all about the names of sailors. However, there are written records of the names of the crew of the *Evangelistria* in 1916: Yiorgos Poéros, Stephanos Chalkidis,

Anastasis Nikola, Savvas Keleshis and his 12-year-old brother Charalambis Michailidis, who was then a deck-hand. A few names are mentioned (though not in full) of the men who worked as sailors on the ships after 1900, e.g. Kostí, Theodosis, Piliettís, Vongos, Mixis, Klavariotis, K. Kouskoutís, Paontís Sekkidis, Loukís Parissis and Karagen.

## Shipowners and Maritime Traders

*Savvas Charalambous (1867–1935)*
A shipowner and active and resourceful merchant from Lefkosia. He married Evanthia Dimitriadi, daughter of Hadji-Gliyóris, and was very active in Kyrenia. At one time he owned up to three vessels: the *Rigaina*, the *Apostolos Andreas*, and the *Evangelistria*, a two-masted schooner weighing 52 tons which was sunk by the French navy on 6 February 1916. It was skippered by Michail Savvas Keleshis. Later, in 1922, together with Demosthenes Severis, he built *Tsiakkiler*, the largest ship ever constructed in Cyprus, with a displacement of 230 tons.

In 1934 he began to construct another ship on Tsiakkilerí that was destined to become the last ever constructed in the town's boatyards. However, it was never completed and was abandoned as an empty shell on the slips. It was bought by Costas Katsellís, who turned it into firewood for his hotel, the Dome.

*Feyim Efendis*
Turkish landowner and wholesale merchant from Kazáfani (1900?).

*Evangelos Evangelidis*
A wholesale merchant from Lefkosia, who owned his own warehouses and a house in the south-western corner of the harbour, which in the 1960s and 70s was owned by the Kyrenia High School Graduates' Association. In the late 19th and early 20th centuries he went into partnership with a number of Kyrenian shipowners.

*Christodoulos Fierós*
A big landowner who is reputed to have engaged in maritime trade.

*The Hadjiouseïnis Brothers*
Turkish merchants from Upper Kyrenia. They dealt mainly in goods from south-east Asia Minor. Their main supplier was Kapetán Fytaís.

*Costas Mitsidis*
The Mitsidis family were wholesale merchants and shipowners from Lefkosia. They owned warehouses in the harbour and shops in Kyrenia and were the largest importers of timber from south-east Asia Minor. Costas Mitsidis owned the large boat *Archángelos*, which weighed almost 100 tons. Shortly before the Second World War the boat was sold to merchants from Turkey.

*Demosthenes Severis*
A wholesale merchant and businessman from Lefkosia who settled in Kyrenia. The biggest shipowner in Cyprus in the early 20th century. At one stage he formed a shipping partnership with Savvas Charalambous. Their last five ships were the *Digenís*, the schooner *Apóstolos Andreas*, the *Buffavento*, the *Chrysokava* and the fleet's flagship, the *Rigaina*, which was more of a passenger ship than a cargo boat. It ran to Alexandria and Beirut. Its last captain was Kapetán Panayís Michailidis. Severis was the largest exporter of carobs in the province and also the last export-trader to use the port of Kyrenia, up until 1954. His large warehouses were situated to the west of the harbour (near the public baths, where he had a private wharf to load the lighters opposite the Dome Hotel). The family funded the construction of the Severis Boys' School (*Sevéreio Arrenagogeío*) in 1912.

*Yiannis (Karákoulles), Michalis and Yiorgos Vasiliou*
Brothers, shipowners and traders. An important Kyrenian family of shipowners who owned the largest ship in the harbour, the three-masted *Tria Adelfia*, which was wrecked outside Smyrna in 1885.